For Jeff

A Wedding to Remember

Switched at Marriage, Episode 1

Gina Robinson

Gina Robinson
SEATTLE, WASHINGTON

CHAPTER ONE

Kayla

I had a bad day. No, scrap that. I had a *hideous* weekend in Reno on business, followed by the crappiest rainy day Monday in the history of Seattle rainy day Mondays. *Ever.* And given our annual total of rainy days, that was saying something. A sad, sob in my double-shot espresso, drag myself to work after a weekend of trying to get over a bad breakup with Eric Monday. The kind of Monday that made me miss the comfort and stresses of college life. The ready availability of friends. And, most of all, easy access to rebound guys. Because even though I worked as a buyer of men's tighty whities and moisture-wicking socks for a small online, and I might add, dying, accessories startup— yeah, men's foundations, exciting! Can you see me rolling my eyes?—men were a rare breed in my industry. Straight men, anyway.

My business degree with a double minor in fashion merchandising and communications was really being put to good use. So much for my dreams of being a buyer for a major Northwest brand.

Eric. I blinked a tear away, or maybe it was a raindrop in my eye. Raindrop. Sure. Why not? But I was deluding myself. In the stages of relationship grief, I was way past shock and denial, and deep into furious-and-feeling-like-a-fool territory.

I dropped my guard, lowered my umbrella, and let myself into my apartment building. At that very moment, the wind kicked up, blowing the water streaming from the eaves directly onto my head and into my part. A cold splash of reality. As if I needed *more* rude awakenings.

Usually the warm familiar friendliness of my West Seattle apartment building perked me up. I loved the hip, energetic vibe of this part of the city. Today my apartment was just shelter from the rain.

Six years worth of off-and-on-again days with Eric since the first time I met him at an Up All Night event my freshman year in college. Back into the off-again stage. *Again.* Only this time felt different. *Permanent.* The douche had ditched me for someone else.

My friends had repeatedly warned me—a guy who can't commit after six years together, especially if the majority of it was in the broken-up phase, wasn't a good bet for the long term. Saying he had to have financial security before he settled down, along with a new motorcycle, a sixty-inch TV, a top-of-the-line snowboard and gear, a new gaming system... You get the idea.

In my defense, I had a lot invested in that relationship. Way too many years to simply give up on him. And hope, terrible, awful hope, clung to me like bad perfume, refusing to fade away.

I shook the rain off my umbrella, stepped inside, and took the elevator to the third floor. I let myself into my dark apartment, flipped the light on, and tossed my keys and soaked purse on the console table in the entryway. Home, sweet home. I was dripping all over it.

I should have known there was a reason Eric kept putting off moving in with me again. Sure, his arguments *seemed* reasonable. I mentally ticked them off like I was counting them on my fingers. One—he wanted to make sure we "stuck" this time before giving up his independence again. Like he'd made so many sacrifices by living with me in the past.

Two—living in my apartment would make his commute too long. Lame excuse, but true. Seattle commutes were killers. And finally, three—he couldn't bail on his roommates. They couldn't afford the house they were renting without him. Also true. And there was no way I was living with that bunch of lazy-ass guys.

But. That hadn't stopped Eric from moving in with *her.* Over the weekend, the bastard. The thought of her gave me an instant case of relationship rage. I took a deep breath. Killing someone right now was not a good idea.

What was he thinking? He and I had a *history* together. We shared a college experience. If I cut him out of my college scrapbook, there would be nothing left but a few shredded ribbons and a picture of the powder puff football trophy my team had won during homecoming my senior year.

I took off my gorgeous pink raincoat, the one that perked me up on dreary Seattle days like this one. My splurge purchase—the coat had cost over five hundred dollars. But it was worth *every* penny. And I mean every one. When I walked down the street wearing it, men looked. And women eyed me with the question *Where did you get that lovely thing?* shining in their eyes. I hung it in the closet and kicked off my soaked shoes.

I'd gone to Reno on Thursday on business to deal with issues at the distribution center for the small apparel firm I kind of worked for. Not exactly the stuff of my fashion merchandizing dreams. And I say "kind of" because my hours kept getting cut. It was just a matter of time before they faded to zero.

I came down with a major case of food poisoning on Friday afternoon, tossed my cookies on the plant manager's shoes, and had to spend an extra day in Reno. Mostly sleeping in the bathtub so I could be near the toilet. Now, on top of everything else, I had a stiff neck. And food still wasn't completely my friend again yet. But I lost three pounds during the adventure. So there was that.

My boss was royally angry about the extra expense. I was mortified by the whole experience. And to top it all off, because, you know, things weren't bad enough, someone had stolen my phone and wallet. They were eventually retrieved from a potted plant in the hotel lobby. Minus my cash, of course. Fortunately, I'd only had one of my two credit cards with me at the time. I'd had to cancel it. But by the time I did, the thief had taken it for a spin and maxed it out. It had been a total pain in the butt trying to pay my hotel bill and get home.

And then Monday hit with a vengeance and the office was no better than Reno. Apparently, the hours-fading-to-zero thing was suddenly on the fast track. They cut my hours. *Again.*

No boyfriend. Barely enough hours to register on the paycheck scale. My life sucked. I figured I was just about at rock bottom. In a weird way, I liked rock bottom. It meant things had to get better. There was just no other way for them to go.

If my life had been a plucky romantic comedy, this was my hero's cue to make his entrance in some totally adorable way. *Hero, where are you?*

I stuck a cup of instant macaroni and cheese in the microwave—cooking for one sucked—and checked the balance of my remaining open credit card on my phone. I crossed my fingers, hoping I had enough credit left to charge my rent. Like everything else in my life, my bank account was pretty much running on empty. My credit card account numbers came up.

"What!" The balance swam before my eyes. "Credit limit exceeded!" I took another deep breath and bit my tongue to hold the curses in. "This can't be right." I blinked. Twice. But, not surprisingly, the numbers didn't change. No matter how hard I wished.

"You weren't even in Reno," I said as if the credit card could hear me, hoping my empty apartment might at least sympathize with the plight we were in. It owed me that much. I'd spent whole paychecks decorating it.

Hands shaking, I brought up my current list of charges.

"Crap!" There were dozens of purchases at shops and casinos in Reno. How had the thief gotten hold of this one, too? I needed one of those identity protection places. Fast. Would they take you after the fact? Why was I never prepared? Oh, yeah, because things like identity theft protection cost money. That I didn't have.

In a panic, I grabbed my purse and dug out my credit card. My hand shook as I held it in front of me and chastised it. "Baby, how could you go shopping without me?"

I sighed. *Rock bottom, where are you?*

I called the credit card company's fraud alert number and explained the situation. Despite my fantastic storytelling, the woman on the other end was not sympathetic. Or even a big believer in my story.

"We'll close the account and investigate the charges. Once we verify they're fraudulent, we'll reverse them and issue you a new card." She paused. "But first, you're going to have to make a payment. You're at your credit limit."

"Wait! What?" I tried to digest the news. "You mean I'm not going to be able to use my card?"

"Correct. Make a payment and we'll do our part." Her voice had that threatening—yet professionally distant and nearly bored—edge to it. "You should have your new card in the mail in ten to fourteen business days. Thanks for using our card and have a nice day."

"But—"

The microwave pinged. The credit card customer service rep hung up. Before I could call her back, my phone buzzed in my hand.

Carl, my building manager. "Kayla, there's a guy down here with a delivery for you."

I frowned. I hadn't ordered anything and Eric was too cheap to mail any stuff I'd inadvertently left with him back.

"Okay." I hedged, trying to avoid direct contact with Carl. "Thanks for the notice. Take it for me, will you? I'll be down for it later."

Carl's next words stopped me as I was halfway to hanging up. "This isn't a courtesy call. The guy won't give it to me."

Carl sounded nervous. Carl never sounded nervous. Nothing bothered him, except people who were late with their rent. And it was looking like I was going to be *very* late this month.

I couldn't ask my parents for the money. I was proving a point that, and damned if I was going to admit defeat. I could be independent and manage a budget just fine, thank you very much. I was not a ditzy, fashion-crazed blond, as they liked to think. Even graduating top in my class at the university didn't dispel their misperceptions. Because, you know, business degrees with double minors were easy to get. In four years. With no extra semesters. Why couldn't I get a real major? Say, engineering. Something scientific. Like my cousin Dex.

Carl's next words snapped me out of my thoughts. "He says he has to give it to you *directly*."

I looked at the microwave. "My dinner's getting cold." Congealed instant mac was the worst. "You can't talk him into just leaving it with you?"

"He doesn't look like the kind of guy you just talk into anything."

Crap. I sighed. "All right. I'm coming. I'll be down in a minute."

I took the elevator to the lobby. Carl and this big guy in a suit were waiting for me. I saw immediately what Carl was talking about. The guy looked like an off-duty bouncer. Not the kind of guy you messed with.

Everything about him was bulging. He was even carrying a bulging legal-size envelope. He turned to Carl. "That her?"

Carl flashed me a look that said he was sorry and gave me up without a fight. "That's her. Kayla Lucas."

I froze. The big guy thrust the envelope into my hands before I could protest. "Kayla Lucas, you've been served."

As I opened my mouth to reply, the big guy turned and strode out the doors at what would have been a sprint for most people, but looked almost leisurely on him.

Now that the threat had walked out the door, Carl went suddenly protective on me. "What's this about?"

I frowned and my heart did a dive for my stomach. "I have no idea."

Carl nodded, looking like he didn't believe me. "If it's about money, I'll cover for you about the rent, Kayla. I can stall the owners for a couple of days. You get paid in a few, right?"

I nodded. I wasn't lying about getting paid, but the reality was my next paycheck was so small it came nowhere near covering what I owed.

"Okay, then." Carl patted me awkwardly on the shoulder. "Let me know if I can help." That was as effusive as Carl got. He was a nice guy, protective of the building's occupants, but mostly unemotional. He cleared his throat and went back to his office.

I took the legal-looking envelope back to my apartment. Why would anyone be serving me for anything? I was basically your law-abiding good girl. I hadn't even had a parking ticket since college. I was totally stumped. I plopped onto my couch.

What if that credit card identity thief in Reno had swindled a casino or something in my name? My fingers shook as I tore the envelope open and read the official-looking documents.

Divorce papers. What—? Was this some cosmic joke?

"Very funny, fate!" I shook the papers, trying to make my point—this was ridiculous. "I'm off men and you know it. I don't even have a boyfriend. And wouldn't take one if you offered me one on a platinum platter." Despite my earlier, ill-timed mention of a hero. "Not even if he was a millionaire boy toy."

I was lying. A millionaire boy toy sounded pretty good right now. I took a deep breath.

"I have a husband. *Riiiight*. And of course, he's a nasty, dumbass, douchebag husband who's divorcing me sight unseen. Probably left me for some airhead. Like Eric did." I was ranting. But it's not like my apartment cared. It was as insensitive as Eric.

This had to be a mistake. Or a crazy joke. Some other Kayla Lucas should probably be receiving this "bad" news. If it really was bad news. Who knew? Maybe this made her happy. Maybe this was what she wanted. But then wouldn't she be the one serving *him*?

I sighed. As far as men went, this really was a crappy day for all the Kayla Lucases of the world. We were being universally dumped. Was there such a thing as a name horoscope? Because it seemed like we were all suffering the same fate at the same time. There had to be some reason to it. *From now through the summer solstice, Kayla Lucases worldwide will be dumped by boyfriends, husbands, and lovers. If none of these exist, a casual flirtation will give you the cold shoulder.*

I raced to my window. Big paper-serving guy was opening the door to a black SUV.

As I opened the window, the rain pelted in. I called out to the server guy over the swoosh of passing traffic kicking up road mist. "You have the wrong Kayla Lucas. I've never even been engaged. My dumbass ex-boyfriend never got the hint he was supposed to propose. This *can't* be me."

He glanced at my building numbers and then up at me. "Right address. Right name. Not my problem." He slid one leg into the SUV.

"Double-check. Please?" I tried batting my eyes at him. But the rain just got in them and gave me an unsightly wink. And my mascara started running just at the wrong time, totally killing my sexy flirt. "You have the *wrong* girl."

He gave me a deadpan, death-eye stare as rain beaded on his dark hair like he was some kind of duck. "Don't blame me. I'm just the messenger." He slid into the SUV and drove away in a cloud of spray.

I slammed my window shut and grabbed the paperwork again. What in the world? Where was rock bottom? I sat down to read the documents more carefully, looking for important details. Like just who was supposed to be divorcing me.

Kayla Lucas, blah blah blah, legalese, legalese. More lawyerly junk. Ah, here we go—Justin Green.

Justin Green? No way! Someone *had* to be pranking me.

"Dex!" I said out loud. "I'll get you for this."

My cousin was known for his epic pranks. He'd vowed to get me back for something I *may* have done to him just before I graduated. I'm not admitting to anything, of course.

Dex was a few years younger than me. We'd gone to the same university. Justin was one of his nerdy, brainiac friends. And now, ironically, given his lack of style, the cofounder of one of the most fashionable, and successful, startups in Seattle, Flashionista.com.

My family was pretty close. I would bet my splurge coat that Dex had already heard about my breakup with Eric. Any time I was depressed about Eric, my mom called his mom to worry about me. They were sisters and about as different as they could be, but very close. Dex, being friends with Justin, was well aware of the crush Justin had had on me in college. And how I hadn't reciprocated it. I thought Justin was terminally sweet, but not my kind of guy. Because my kind of guy, apparently, was a douchebag.

Justin and I had the world's tiniest past, if you can even call one class in college a past. He was a skinny, short, gawky, geeky guy who looked too young to be out of junior high, let alone away at college by himself. The guys made fun of him. And picked on him. Bullied him, really. But he was genius smart and managed to get back at them in very clever ways. Which I secretly admired.

Dex, who was a geek boy himself, teased me about Justin being my boyfriend. Dex's words came back to haunt me. "Give it up! If you were smart, you would take advantage of his misplaced affection for you and marry him, Lala. I think he has potential. Maybe he'll even grown an inch or two so you can wear your prized heels around him."

Even though I was only five foot five, in heels, I towered over poor Jus. I remembered rolling my eyes and laughing at Dex. "My height doesn't bother me. I'm confident being taller than the guy."

Dex shook his head like he didn't believe me. "Uh-huh. That explains Eric and all the dumb, tall jocks you go for. Take it from your cousin, who loves you, baby, Justin's going to be rich. Obscenely rich. You spend like there's no tomorrow. You're going to need a husband who's loaded. Better get him now before his money makes him irresistible."

I hadn't believed in Dex's prophetic abilities. Until Justin struck it rich in the online flash sale industry and became a billionaire last month when the company went public. I'd read about it on the news.

The thing was, I would have loved to work at Flashionista. They were cutting-edge trendsetters. Their buyers were ahead of the curve, spotting what would soon be hot and capitalizing on it while prices were still affordable. They sold the absolute hottest, got-to-have boutique, and commercial, fashions in their daily flash sales. For unbelievably low prices. If you weren't on their site at six a.m. when the deals went live, you missed the best stuff.

I had the knack. I could do it, too. They were growing like crazy. I would love to work as buyer for them. Half of my generation of Seattleites wanted to work there, especially those, like me, for whom fashion merchandising was a passion. I may have mentioned it to Dex.

I cocked an eyebrow. "Ha ha, Dex. You think you are *so* funny!"

This was epic, as he would say. He'd gone to a lot of trouble, I gave him that much credit. The legal documents looked genuine. But then, you can get legal documents on any number of websites. And the big paper-serving guy? Dex could afford to pay him to play the part. His dad was loaded.

Justin Green, the most eligible nerd in Seattle, billionaire boy genius, divorcing me was a prank only someone like Dex would think up. Damn him! I was going to get him back.

When I'd been in class with Justin, I'd been lost in the middle of my two thousand days with Eric. So totally, stupidly, preoccupied with Eric that I barely noticed any other guy. But, to be honest, even if there had been no Eric, I wouldn't have noticed Justin. As I said, he wasn't the kind of guy girls drooled over, as superficial as that sounded.

I tried to suppress a grin, and lost. Then I broke out into a full-blown smile. My shoulders shook. I covered my mouth with my hands as a giggle escaped. I mean, how could I laugh at a time like this? My world was completely in the toilet.

My sides started shaking. I wrapped my arms around myself, but I still couldn't hold it in. A laugh escaped. And another. I laughed. And laughed. And laughed until my sides hurt and my eyes watered. Until tears ran down my cheeks and I felt better than I had in months.

I wiped my cheeks and eyes with the back of my hand and fell over on the couch, with the divorce papers shaking in my hand.

I was tempted to get on Twitter and hashtag JustinGreen, hashtag divorce. Hashtag ha ha very funny.

I wiped my eyes with the back of my hand again. "Focus, Kay."

I forced myself to read more and see how far this prank went. Because Dex never did anything by half. This should be rich. I was being summoned to the law offices of pompous lawyer and so and so tomorrow morning at ten. To talk about a settlement before they filed the divorce petition officially with the court. Never even having been married, I had no idea how divorces worked. This could be complete BS.

But it was politely worded. *Please text your response if I can make it. Or call the office at your earliest convenience to reschedule.*

I was also under orders to keep this whole divorce under wraps or risk losing any potential settlement. Of course Dex would want it kept quiet.

If Dex was going to these elaborate lengths, I was game for playing along. Even if it meant I showed up at some random law office Dex had picked off the Internet and got blank stares. An adventure would be a pleasant diversion. And give the family a good laugh at Christmas. If anyone in that law office had a sense of humor, they'd laugh with me, too.

I whipped out my phone and texted my reply—*I'll be there.* I almost added, *and I'll be expecting male strippers. At the very least a surprise party.* Though it wasn't anywhere near my birthday.

With my hours being cut to nearly nothing, I had the day off anyway. I may as well go downtown and do some window-shopping or stop by the market and get some flowers or a cheesecake bite on a stick. Dipped in chocolate. Hmmm...good news! My appetite was coming back.

I was even in the mood to watch the guys at the market throw fish. Dex knew how to get to me. And pick up my spirits. Always had. And I never bailed on a challenge as delicious as the one he'd just issued.

Justin

It was past seven in the evening, but I was still in the office, staring at the screen of my desktop. I should have been working, but I was too deep into self-punishment and loathing.

Shit. I was up to my knees in it and damage control. Riggins, my business partner, was going to kill me if this marriage mistake screwed with the company.

I frowned, trying to remember pesky details, like what Kayla had looked like at our impromptu Reno wedding. But it was a blank. A total void. Like a scene from *The Hangover.*

A knock on my office door startled me from my self-flagellation.

Harry Lawrence, my legal counsel and friend, stuck his head in. "Got a minute? I have news."

"Yeah. Come in." My heart raced. I hoped the news was good. But what the hell constituted good in this situation? I was at a loss.

Harry slid into the office and closed the door. "We found her. She's been served and agreed to our meeting tomorrow morning."

I studied Harry, looking for clues in his expression. "That was fast. Where was she?"

"Her apartment in West Seattle."

I nodded. West Seattle felt like a place the Kayla I remembered would live. "What did she say?"

I was pissed and hurt and embarrassed. I had to know why the hell she'd run out on me.

Harry shrugged. "That's it. Everything I know. She said she'd be here." Harry hesitated. "Marrying her without a prenup was a real fuckup."

I nodded. "Do you have the paperwork drawn up?"

Harry had been the first person I'd called after I realized my mistake. The only person. If Harry couldn't fix this, no one could.

"Justin, as your lawyer, I have to caution you—this is dangerous. It could backfire in your face is so many ways. And it's going to cost you millions. Is this what you really want?"

I flipped my hand casually, like I didn't give a damn about a couple million. Compared to what was at stake, it was peanuts. "It's only a matter of time before someone uncovers the record of the marriage. A divorce is going to be a matter of public record, as well.

"Reporters, my competitors, they're always trying to dig shit up on me. Divorcing days after getting married will look flaky and irresponsible to the analysts, investors, and market. I can't risk driving stock prices down so soon after the IPO. I just need to flush her out and talk to her. Give her my proposal."

Harry looked damnably sympathetic for a guy who got any girl he wanted. "This could backfire in your face. She ran out on you after less than twelve hours of marriage. What makes you think she's reliable?"

"Cold feet are common enough." I set my jaw.

"But not usually on the wedding night." He sounded like he was arguing the case against her, or me, in court.

"Most people don't get married after a few hours, either." I wouldn't be deterred.

"What makes you think she'll stay and play the part? Keep her mouth shut now?"

"She's on the rebound from that douche Eric. She'll want to show him."

Harry frowned. "She sounds petty."

I stared Harry down, irrationally angry and defensive for her. "She sounds human."

Harry's eyes narrowed like he was trying to pin me down and win this case. "You're asking her to give up a hell of a lot. Freedom is no small thing."

"Give me liberty or give me death?" I laughed, but it was bitter. "Only for a year. Maybe less. Everything has a price. The Kayla I knew wasn't a swindler. But she likes nice things. She's shrewd. She knows the value of a good deal. I only want one thing. I need you to ask her why she left." I paused in thought.

"Will that make a difference?" Harry sounded puzzled.

He didn't understand and I didn't expect him to. But he had a point—would it?

"Maybe." I sighed. "We've done our due diligence on her. It's an acceptable risk."

Harry hadn't stopped frowning. "You're the client. Just make damn sure you don't combine any assets or you're screwed. This is a community property state."

"If you've done your job, the contract is airtight. It won't be a problem. We offered her an enticement, a bonus at the end if she keeps her mouth shut and doesn't cause trouble for us?" I always double-checked.

Harry nodded. "We'll tell her that if she ends this now, she gets nothing. The courts won't take her abandonment lightly. We have a strong case against her. I've written in the allowance you specified."

I nodded again. "We'll keep her under tabs. Everything will be fine, Harry. Trust me."

Now if I could just convince myself.

CHAPTER TWO

Kayla

I wasn't sure how to dress to get divorced. Or pranked.
My fashion choice was complicated by the shopping I
planned to do afterward. Having been recently
dumped, I decided that any respectable girl on the edge
of divorce, prank or otherwise, would dress to show her
ex *exactly* what he was missing. I dressed like I was
showing *Eric* what *he* was missing. He was the douchebag I really wanted revenge on.

I took special care with my hair and makeup. I did
everything I could think of to make myself feel good.
And powerful. And sexy. Including using my new mascara product that put lash fibers on my eyelashes to
make them look smoking. Because lashes that jump off
the page really get the guys, apparently. At least ac-

cording to beauty product commercials. I wanted to watch his Adam's apple bob when I batted my eyes and refused to pucker my lips for him. Or maybe that was actually Eric I was thinking of.

I dressed in my new outfit—flouncy skirt, a white lace cami, and navy suit jacket with brass buttons and a ruffled edge as a nod to the "seriousness" of the occasion. I added the new platform pumps I'd gotten for a steal off the Flashionista website. He was a guy. Would he notice? It was probably a wasted effort.

He would notice, however, when I towered over him. I laughed at myself. Poor Jus. Eric had really done me wrong.

I was ready for a day of any, or all, of the following: divorcing, outing pranks, and shopping. On the bright side, maybe I'd get lucky and get some alimony from this adventure—ha ha! I was hoping for at least lunch on Dex.

It was June and the sun was shining, which only minimally picked my spirits up. As furious as I was at Eric, I was still mourning him. I grabbed my flowered tote, stuffed the bogus legal papers in it, and took the bus to downtown Seattle.

This was crazy, really stupidly crazy. But at least the divorce had taken my focus off Eric.

Oh, Dex, I thought with a smile on my face.

I got off the bus a block away and made it to the law offices with five minutes to spare. Their offices were on the fourteenth floor. Expensive real estate. The décor was modern, tasteful, elegant. And intimidating. I suspected intentionally.

I bet myself this was a real law office with no idea what was going on. Dex was good. The lawyer's name, Harry Lawrence, was even on the door.

I took a deep breath. Inside, I introduced myself to the efficient-looking woman at the reception desk, expecting a blank look. "Kayla Lucas. I have an appointment with Harry Lawrence?" I winked at her.

She stared back at me with professional lack of humor. "Mr. Lawrence and Mr. Green are waiting for you in the conference room. They left instructions to show you right in." She stood. "This way."

I stared at her. Okay, Dex was taking this farther than I thought he would. The law office, or at least the receptionist, was in on it.

"He's *really* expecting *me*?" I pointed to myself. "Kayla Lucas?" I tagged after her as she strode confidently ahead.

"Of course." She pushed a door open ahead of me and poked her head in. "Ms. Lucas to see you." She stepped back out of the way and held the door to let me in.

I braced myself for a surprise. Male strippers. Clowns. I hated clowns. They scared me. And Dex knew it. Which is exactly why I wouldn't put it past him. Friends jumping up to yell, "Surprise!"

Maybe hidden cameras to catch the whole thing for a YouTube video. *Girl divorced by man she never married.* Could be a YouTube sensation. If it went viral I could bask in my fifteen minutes of fame.

I took a deep breath and plunged into the room. The receptionist shut the door quietly behind me. I was supremely disappointed—no friends, no clowns.

Unless you counted the two men who sat quietly at a conference table. I didn't recognize either of them. One wore a baggy, unfashionable sports coat that was too big for his slender frame, jeans, and tennis shoes. His back was to me as he looked out the window. I couldn't see his face, just the back of his head. He was tall. His dark hair was unruly and needed a cut.

The other was dressed in a tailored suit that fit him as neatly as second skin. He was clean-shaven, well built, dark, and, even at a slight distance, smelled good, like expensive cologne and scented soap, as he stood and came toward me. If one of these two was going to be a stripper, I hoped it was the guy in the suit.

The suit extended his hand. "Harry Lawrence." His voice was cool and professional, but tight, like he was holding back his anger. Or maybe his laughter. He looked past me as if he was looking for someone or something.

I looked around him, expecting Dex to pop up and my friends to jump out of nowhere. But the conference room was sparsely furnished. There was no place for them to be hiding. I was on my own here.

I felt the sudden prickling of anxiety. This scene felt serious and official. Not at all like a prank. Either these guys were ready for a major acting award, or they'd made a mistake. Maybe Dex had paid them extra to give me a supremely good scare? If that was the case, it was working. I was losing my confidence in the idea this was one of his pranks.

"Kayla." I tried not to sound as uncertain as I felt as I offered my name, shook the suit's hand, and joined him in looking around. "Am I missing something?" I put just a hint of flirt in my tone. He was good looking. So what that I was off men? I wasn't dead.

"Where's your lawyer?" Harry's gaze held mine a second too long before he looked behind me again.

I smiled at him and gave him a conspiratorial look. "Okay, Mr. Lawrence—"

"Call me Harry."

"Happily. Harry"—I winked at him and pulled the divorce papers from my bag—"the game is over. Did Dex put you up to this stunt?" I shook the papers and slapped them on the table with a flourish, wondering if now he'd at least take off his suit jacket.

"I hate to contradict you, but the game is just beginning." His eyes snapped like he was eagerly anticipating a good battle. "Who's Dex?"

"Give it up," I said, ignoring his question. "This is a joke."

"You call scamming my client a joke? What do you want, Kayla? You married Justin without a prenup. I'm sure that was by design—get a guy drunk. Con him into marrying you. Fleece him big time?" He raised one eyebrow.

I laughed. "Awesome. That is a really good story. You should write a novel." I took a deep breath. "But I have to warn you. There's been a mistake—"

I didn't even see Justin anywhere.

Harry didn't look even a *little* bit amused. Which was too bad, because this was hilarious. And I liked a man who liked to laugh. Some people had no sense of humor. Like lawyers.

"You have no claim on Justin's assets or any part of Flashionista." He looked and sounded totally serious. And he still had all his clothes on.

I stared at him as if he were crazy. Because he was. Practically certifiable. He was talking utter, complete, stupid nonsense. "Stop kidding. The prank's over. This is losing its funny."

He wasn't even flirting back with me now. Suddenly he'd gone serious cop on me.

"Kidding?" Harry pointed to the guy staring out the window. "You targeted and conned my client. Married him under false pretenses. And ran out on him. You call that a prank?"

I stared at him. He was dead serious.

"No, I call that heartless. Whoever did it should be ashamed. But it wasn't *me*. The real Justin would know that I would never do something to hurt him like that. I like him. He's sweet." I pointed at the guy staring out the window. "That isn't even Justin Green. Not the one *I* knew. Dex screwed up. He should have hired a shorter actor."

The guy looking out the window was too tall and mature. And yet...

"If any of this is true, you have the wrong person." I spoke boldly, but I was wavering. There *was* something familiar about the guy with his back to me.

Harry held his hand up to stop my protests. "You don't have to keep asserting your innocence. We have a business proposition for you." Harry glanced at the guy who was still staring out the window. "It's a generous offer. I suggest you consider it carefully and take it before he changes his mind."

He cleared his throat. "But first, my client wants to know one thing—why did you desert him without an explanation?"

"*I* didn't desert him. And I don't want his money." The words popped out automatically.

I should have been tempted. I needed the money. Like, really needed it. But I wasn't going to jump at a joke. Dex would think that was too funny. I'd never hear the end of it. And if this wasn't a joke? I hadn't married him. I wasn't the one.

"When are you going to listen to me? I never married your supposed client." I looked at the guy now, too.

The supposed Justin was still staring out the window as if his alleged divorce proceedings weren't going on in the room around him. His shoulders were square. In fact, he was so still, he radiated with quiet anger. In my experience, that's the worst kind.

"If this really isn't a prank, I'm not the Kayla Lucas you're looking for. You've got the wrong Kayla." I clutched my tote tightly against me and turned to leave. "I've had enough. I'm out of here."

Harry wouldn't let it go. "Maybe you don't remember?"

I stopped in my tracks and turned around. "Don't remember? How do you *not* remember getting married?"

"Kayla, please. Let's stop the innocent act. We know you were in Reno last weekend staying at the same hotel as Justin." Harry pulled some papers from a stack on the table and held them out to me. "Your marriage license. Dated last Friday night." He tapped one of the papers. "That's your signature."

"What?" I snatched the paper away and gasped. The paper was an authentic-looking marriage license. The signature looked enough like mine to make me sweat.

Just then the guy in the chair swiveled around and faced me. "I don't. Remember getting married." His voice was deep and sexy, the kind of voice that belonged on the radio. When his eyes met mine, his brow furrowed.

The guy in the chair had a bushy beard and mustache. It was more than just Seattle style. It was like he thought he was a hipster or something. He was stockier than I remembered Justin being, more filled out, taller and better built. But his eyes were Justin's. Sensitive. Innocent in an endearing way. But shining with hurt he was obviously trying to control.

"Justin?" I was tentative and unsure, still not one hundred percent confident I wasn't being pranked by an imposter. "Is that *really* you?"

Beneath the baggy sports coat, he was wearing a band T-shirt. The shirt looked suspiciously like an oversize one he'd had in college. Only he filled this one out much better than he used to. I knew for certain now—he was Justin Green.

I frowned, completely puzzled. "What is this all about, Justin? Did Dex put you up to this? Tell Harry I *didn't* marry you."

Harry turned to Justin for confirmation.

Justin shook his head almost imperceptibly. "I can't, Kay. I really don't remember. That license says we did."

Justin

The sight of Kayla made my breath catch. Just like it had at the hotel in Reno when I'd caught a glimpse of her. She was even hotter than my smoking adolescent college memories of her. I fought the old feelings of gawky insecurity and inferiority. Being near her again made my palms sweat. Crap, even my heart sweat.

This was Kayla, *the* Kayla I remembered. Natural blond hair. Sparkling lilac eyes. And genuine surprise and delight at seeing me. Right then, I would have done anything to stop her from walking out that door. *Ever.* I knew I'd made the right decision.

Kayla's frown deepened. "Don't remember?"

She was gorgeous when she was puzzled. She paled. "I *was* in Reno last weekend. But I didn't even see you. Let alone marry you. I had no idea you were there, too." Her eyes begged me to explain. "I spent most of my time in my hotel room, puking."

Her words were flippant and self-deprecating, amused. Anyone else would have been embarrassed. Not Kayla. She was always incredibly plucky.

If I imagined hard enough, she was even a little flirty. But that was just her being her, too. "Ah-hah, Kay. See? Drunk? Weren't we both?"

As she shook her head, her hair swung gently. She brushed a curl out of her face. "Not drunk. A horrific case of food poisoning. A bad piece of fish at lunch, I think. Enough to make me very sick."

"You disappoint me," I said.

She laughed again, nervously now, studying me like I was nearly a complete stranger. Like she didn't really believe it was me. Like the marriage stuff was complete crap. "You're not joking? You really think we got married?"

I prompted her. "I was in Reno for business. While I was checking in, I spotted you in the hotel lobby. I waved, but you didn't see me. I took a chance you hadn't changed your number since college, texted you, and asked you out for a drink Friday night." I tried to keep my tone neutral and not let my foolish crush on her show. I pulled my phone from my pocket, brought up her texts, and handed it to Harry to hand to her to see. "Here's our conversation. We met for drinks—"

"No!" She shook her head as she took it from me. "I never got a text from you. I'm positive. And by Friday night, I was so sick, I had to cancel my flight home and hang around another day. My boss was furious at having to foot the bill. I didn't leave my hotel room until early Saturday morning. I didn't have the energy."

She frowned prettily as she looked at the texts she'd sent me.

Then suddenly, she paled again. "Oh, crap." She took a deep breath and swayed on her feet. "This is crazy. Someone stole my purse and phone Friday. I got them back later from the hotel. Someone had ditched them in a planter. A hotel employee found them and returned them to me. You don't think..."

I stared at her, waiting for her to finish.

Always the hero, Harry caught her elbow and pulled a chair out for her before I could move. She plopped into it, looking seriously stunned.

The best I could do was push a bottle of water toward her in a feeble, late-breaking attempt at gallantry. "Drink this. You look pale."

She stared at the water bottle as if it were a foreign object, and handed my phone back. "It's totally farfetched, but someone charged a boatload of clothes and junk on my credit card. You don't think someone was more than stealing my identity? That they were pretending to be me? Could someone have fooled you into thinking she was me?"

"No!" I uncapped the bottle for her and held it out to her. "No one could fool me. I would recognize you anywhere, any time."

She had to understand. I meant it. She was the one girl who was permanently etched in my mind. It was key. I couldn't lose her now.

"I got hammered when you didn't show up." Damn, how had that slipped out? "But even drunk, I would have known you." I frowned.

Kayla looked away quickly, as if I'd embarrassed her. She grabbed her bag and rummaged through it.

"You can't even remember the wedding. Where's my phone?"

Harry took a seat and took charge. "We have the piece of paper to prove two people using your names and signatures got married. I don't like this, Justin." He paused. "And a witness of questionable credibility from the twenty-four-hour wedding chapel. He claims two people matching your descriptions got married Saturday night. He showed me a copy of the official license they filed with the state of Nevada."

I barely heard Harry as I watched Kayla carefully.

"Ah! Here it is." Kayla pulled her phone from her tote and looked through her texts. She gasped. "You're right! You did text, Jus, but I never got them. And someone texted you back, but it wasn't me." She turned the phone around for Harry and me to see, still looking stunned and like she was trying to process the situation. "That's so random and bizarre. This really *isn't* a prank?"

I shook my head, fighting my anger. "Not by me. Someone is screwing with us."

Embarrassed? Humiliated? There wasn't a word strong enough to describe how I felt just then. It was like running through a room naked. With a boner, because I was incredibly turned on by her. My inner fantasies, my inner self, had just been exposed. Mix that with rage and I was about to explode. What if this was a ploy by one of our competitors to discredit me? Or somehow steal our company-proprietary algorithms? I clenched my fist and took a deep breath.

Yeah, Kayla had to know I'd had a crush on her as a dumb seventeen-year-old who felt like a misfit at college. Now I'd just tipped my hand that it had been more than a crush. I'd fallen in love with Kayla in a desperate, first-love way I couldn't shake. She had to see now that I'd never gotten over her.

"I called the credit card company," she said in a stunned voice. "Canceled the card and reported the charges as false. I never dreamed..." She looked to Harry for help.

Of course she looked to Harry. All the girls did. Handsome, hot, frat-boy Harry. Just what all the former sorority babes like Kayla wanted.

"This is crazy. What do we do now?" Her eyes were wide, and flashed with anger. "We can't let her get away with it. She somehow engineered this fake marriage using our names and identities. What's her game? What does she want?"

Shit, I never wanted Kayla more than I did at that moment. I wanted her eyes to flash with outrage on my behalf now and forever.

Harry looked to me for direction. "Justin? We need a word."

I shook my head. "This doesn't change anything. We proceed with the original plan. It's even more important now."

Kayla jumped in. "We have to stop her! What if she comes back at Justin and tries to blackmail him out of more? What if she demands a huge alimony settlement or something?" Even when she frowned she was gorgeous. When she turned her lilac eyes on me, I went to mush.

"The bitch." Her gaze slid down me, measuring the changes. "I don't get why she ran out on you."

For a second, my heart jumped and my hopes soared. *She likes what she sees!*

All that time at the gym each day with a personal trainer was paying off.

Until she continued, with a pretty furrow in her brow, "Maybe she didn't realize the opportunity she had. Maybe she didn't know who you are and what she could have gotten out of you."

If Kayla was faking her innocence, she was doing a damned good job. I crashed back to reality. "Yeah, maybe. Harry, I need a quick word with you. Alone."

CHAPTER THREE

Kayla

Harry pushed back from the table. I was intrigued now by the whole situation.

"This is the damnedest divorce meeting I've ever seen," Harry said as he stood.

"Like that's a big deal. You're a contract lawyer, not a divorce attorney. How many have you seen?" Justin shot back as he stood, too.

The way he was able to tease at a time like this was completely adorable. Eric would have flipped and flown into a rage. Justin kept his calm and his sense of humor while I was freaking out inside.

Harry shook his head as if he couldn't believe what was going on. "You wanted a contract lawyer on this. I consulted the firm's hotshot divorce attorney. We can bring him in on this."

Justin joined him at the door. He was even taller than I had imagined when he was sitting. His shoulders were broader. His new confidence was surprising and a relief. What had happened to the scrawny, insecure guy he used to be? If he dressed in clothes that fit him, he might actually not be too bad to look at. I could barely believe this was the same Justin I'd known in college.

"We'll just be a minute," Justin said. "If you need anything, let Laura at reception know." Then he and Harry stepped outside.

They were gone about ten minutes, leaving me to imagine all sorts of schemes. What was that identity thief's game? What had the bitch wanted? She obviously wasn't too bright, letting a billionaire go. And marrying him under a false identity. If she'd used her real name, the marriage would probably have been legal.

I shuddered at the thought of her taking Justin for half his billions. She was still a threat. What if she realized who he really was and sold her story to the tabloids? Or blackmailed him?

Justin came back alone. "I asked Harry to wait for me outside. I wanted to talk to you alone now."

I jumped at the sound of his voice.

"Sorry to startle you." His smile was sympathetic.

"No, it's okay. I was lost in thought. Is it just me? Or is this wild and weird? And a little like something out of an episode of *Dateline*?"

"No one's died," he said.

"Good point. We don't want to add murder to the mix. But disappearing women?"

He laughed softly. "It's not you. It's definitely both, with a little of 'What the shit' thrown in."

I couldn't wrap my head around any of it—the way he'd changed and the situation we were in. Someone pretending to be me and duping Justin into marriage was either a better prank than even Dex could have thought up or a diabolical scheme. Or complete stupidity.

"You've changed." I rubbed my chin, and mimed an imaginary pointed beard. "What's with this?"

The Justin of old had been baby-faced.

He took a seat next to me at the table and turned his chair so he faced me. "Because I can. And it makes me look older. I can't run a company constantly being mistaken for a twelve-year-old."

I slid my gaze over him. "No one's going to mistake you for a boy now."

He smiled and hesitated, as if he was searching for words. "This whole situation is...embarrassing." His gaze held mine. "Kayla, this dumb shit stunt of mine puts me and my company in a bad situation. I need a favor, a *big* favor, from you. You're the only one who can help me." He laughed at himself. "It's bad negotiating technique to lead with that. But it's true."

I stared at him, heart pounding as he took my hands in his. His were surprisingly large and warm. Mine had gone ice cold in the overactive air conditioning.

"I didn't think I'd ever be proposing to a girl like this...proposing something like this." He took a deep breath. "I need you...I would be very...grateful...if you would stay married to me."

My mouth fell open. I knew I was gaping, but I couldn't make my mouth or voice work.

"Not forever. Just for...a year. I'm willing to compensate you—generously—for your trouble."

I felt my mouth working like a fish's. Open. Close. Open. Close. But no sound came out at first. "But we aren't...but I never—"

"It's legal enough as long as we both claim it's real. We have a witness. You were holed up in your hotel room. No one saw you. The facts fit. If that identity thief bitch ever shows up, it will be her word against...ours. Who will the courts and public believe?"

There was a second, maybe even a half a second, when the thought crossed my mind. *He doesn't believe I'm telling the truth about not marrying him. He thinks I'm trying to get out of it.*

I brushed the thought aside, too stunned by the turn of events to think clearly. "I...don't know. It would be complicated. To say the least."

"I know." He nodded. "But we can handle it. I wouldn't ask if it weren't vital. I have nearly a thousand people depending on me for their livelihood. I can't let them down."

He began explaining about his company. How important it was to him and how he had to look responsible. How being scammed would make his investors lose confidence in him and, more importantly, the company. About how we could shut down the identity thief before she came back and tried to do more damage. Made demands that could ruin him and Flashionista. Or tried to claim the marriage was legit. Something about more money if that's what I wanted.

I listened, but didn't hear. It was too much to take in until he mentioned money. "I don't want your money. I stand on my own two feet and earn my way in life."

He squeezed my hands, looking inordinately pleased. "Think of being my wife like a job. You'll have to act the part. All the time. Go to charity events. Be seen in public with me. Travel with me. It will be a hell of a lot of work. You'll definitely earn your money. What can I do to convince you?"

"I don't prostitute myself."

He blushed. "I don't expect sex."

I didn't know whether to be relieved or hurt by his quick answer. I hated to admit it, but apparently I was one of those shallow girls who wanted a guy to lust after her. Forever. I know, irrational. But, you know, every girl wants to be desired when she's being proposed to. As it turns out, that's true even if the marriage is faked.

I took a deep breath. "I'm not ready to be married—"

"According to this." He picked up the license. "You already are."

I took a deep breath, willing myself to think. I *was* intrigued. "What kind of arrangement are you proposing? Would we live together, for example?"

"Most married people do. It will make the charade more convincing. That's essential."

"But what will everyone think? What will *my parents* think?" I shuddered at the thought. "Eric and I just broke up. I'm off men. It will be a hard sell."

"Eric? The same Eric from college?" He sounded surprised.

"Yeah, unfortunately. I'm a stupid sucker for him." I corrected myself: "I *was* a stupid sucker for him." Maybe that sounded a little too fierce.

"I'm sorry." He was trying to look sympathetic, but I saw through him. He'd never liked Eric.

"It's okay. *Really*. I'm better off without him." Or so I kept telling myself.

"He's a real douchebag for letting you get away." He sounded genuine about that, at least.

"That's nice of you to say. On the bright side, it makes things less complicated for us." I reached into my tote for a tissue.

As I dabbed my eyes, I looked at Justin, trying to imagine him as my husband. And realizing with a shock that now that he was a billionaire and I was just one broke girl, he was out of *my* league. The world was on its ear. Girls the world over would die to be in my place right now. I had to save my dignity.

"You'll look like rebound guy. Like I just married you to show him. 'See, I married a billionaire—ha ha! In your face, sucker.' You could have anyone, any girl you wanted now. Do you really want to be *my* rebound guy?"

He got a funny look on his face. "I would be honored to be your *any* kind of guy."

I laughed. "And given your situation, you really don't have any choice."

He grinned, looking like I'd called his bluff.

I thought out loud. "I'll look like a mercenary bitch. Everyone will think I married you for your money."

"So? What the hell do we care?" His eyes snapped and he sounded fierce. "Let them. We'll know, I'll know, the real reason. You have a good heart. You're helping out a friend. You're taking a challenging temporary assignment."

Crap. He was wearing me down.

"Pets?" I asked.

"I have a dog," he said. "You?"

I shook my head. "Kids?" I grinned. Someone had to lighten the tone.

"I thought you said no sex?" There was a tease in his voice. "Maybe if we make it past the one-year mark—"

I rolled my eyes. "I meant, do you currently have any?"

"Is that a deal breaker?" His eyes sparkled.

"Absolutely."

"Having them or not? Because I can adopt."

I grinned. "I like childless men."

He grinned back.

I couldn't believe I was actually considering his strange arrangement. "The thing is—logistics," I said. "I told Mom I was sick over the weekend. I told my coworkers. I made a fabulous story out of it and got a lot of sympathy." I tried to smile. "I mean, a lot. Am I a pathological liar now? Why would I lie to them?"

"Because you wanted to announce the wonderful news in person. And a case of food poisoning is the perfect cover for an elopement."

I'd forgotten what a great sense of humor he had. I frowned. "Except...I threw up all over the plant manager's shoes at the distribution site for the company I sort of work at."

"Nerves," he said. "Pre-wedding jitters. Happens all the time."

I frowned. I had to remind him of one final slip-up, even though it could cost me a literal fortune. "There's a hitch—I called the credit card company. Remember?"

"No problem. I'll have my people call them and tell them you were mistaken about the charges. I'll pay the bill in full." He paused. "How much do you owe?"

"Now you ask?" I teased. "Pocket change to you. About three thousand."

"Done." He looked relieved. "I'll get you signed up with one of those identity protection services. We don't want any problems with your impersonator."

I was still wavering.

"A fake marriage is serious stuff," he said. "If you need time to think it over, I'll understand. But think of it this way, Kay, it could be a grand adventure."

I looked into his eyes. He was dead serious. And he'd been thinking what I had. When would I get the chance to be a billionaire's wife again?

"I work a lot. I won't be home much. You can do pretty much anything you want, as long as you keep our secret and don't publicly embarrass me...with other men." He stared down at our clasped hands and rubbed mine with his thumb. "For my part, I promise to put the toilet seat down and pick up my socks. Well, the maid picks up my socks. But same deal, right?"

"Are you saying we're not going to have an open marriage of convenience?" I shook my head. "Crap, that sounds old-fashioned."

"You believe in open marriages?" He looked surprised.

"I meant the marriage of convenience thing—who does that?"

He laughed. It was a heartwarming, melodious sound.

"What about you?" I said. "I don't want to be embarrassed, either. Are you giving up a girlfriend?"

He looked startled by the question. "I work too much to have a girlfriend."

"But a wife is no problem?"

His grin deepened. "A wife of convenience. They're much more understanding. Girlfriends expect too much."

I smiled back at him. My life was pretty much in the toilet. What did I have to lose? Still, it was a huge deal to rush into marriage, even a highly convenient one. "Can I sleep on it?"

He nodded. "Harry's drawing up a contract. Take it with you. Read it over. Get a lawyer to look at it for you."

"I need a lawyer now, too?" I said.

"It's your standard post-nup," he said in an amused voice. "But yeah. Always have a lawyer look over the fine print."

"Post-nup?" I laughed at the absurdity.

His expression became serious, all business suddenly. "It guarantees you ten million dollars, flat rate, if you keep your end of the bargain, and an amicable divorce for both of us at the end of a year."

I studied him. His bushy beard needed a trim. Actually, it needed to either be cut off entirely or cut very close. His hair was a mess. On impulse, I reached up and smoothed down a piece of his hair that was sticking up at an odd angle. He was not my type. So why was my heart racing? The money? The sense of adventure? I didn't trust my motives. Maybe I *was* a moneygrubbing bitch.

He looked startled by my touch.

I dropped my hand as if I'd committed a sin and cleared my throat. "I'll text you my answer in the morning."

CHAPTER FOUR

Justin

Despite my total screw-up, everything was falling into place. I almost had a hot wife. I *would* have her. I needed her.

Harry returned to the conference room and handed Kayla a sheaf of legal documents.

Kayla took them, stuffed them into her tote, and stood to leave. "It was good to see you again, Justin. Nice to meet you, Harry." She slipped her tote over her shoulder. "See you around. You'll have my answer in the morning." She turned her back to me and walked out the door before I could respond.

I watched her go, hoping I'd done the right thing.

Harry whistled when she was out of sight. "That girl is a stunner."

"Shut up. That's my wife you're ogling."

"Not yet."

"Isn't she?" I stared at him. "I have the license and the witnesses to prove it."

"You're counting your chickens."

"She won't leave me," I said. "There's no way in hell I'm letting her go. There's too much at stake."

Kayla

By the time I left the law offices, it was almost noon and my stomach was growling. The day was gorgeous and sunny blue. It was true. The bluest skies *were* in Seattle. Or maybe they only looked that way in contrast to two hundred drab, gray days a year. Maybe the skies were just as blue in California. But not nearly as appreciated. And maybe my life had just taken a blue-sky-day turn for the better. It had certainly gotten a whole lot more interesting.

I walked to Pike Place Market as a gentle breeze blew in off Puget Sound, catching my skirt and blowing it up nearly around my waist. A breeze always blew downtown. I laughed and clamped my skirt down around my thighs as I walked.

I could be rich. A simple flick of the pen and I wouldn't have to worry about money for the rest of my life. *Independence, here I come! No one will tell me what to do.* The next year, however, was a different story. How much was a year of pretending worth?

Could I really live with Justin? For a whole year? I'd never had much luck with roommates. Or living with guys. Then again, as far as guys went, I'd only ever lived with Eric. Maybe he wasn't the best example.

What would I tell my parents? My friends? How would I explain things? How would I explain the marriage and the divorce when I finally met a guy I really wanted to marry? What if I never met that guy? What if I met him during the year of playing Justin's wife?

The whole situation felt unreal.

On the other hand, if I turned down the money, would I always regret it? More than the money, was this the adventure I'd always dreamed of? A way out of a life of ordering moisture-wicking boxer briefs for a living?

No matter what happened, I felt rich already. But for today my luxuries were simple—a bouquet from the Market and a cup of rich, delicious Beecher's mac and cheese for lunch. My mouth watered at the thought.

The Market hummed with its usual active buzz and busy tourist traffic. The fish throwers were tossing salmons with their usual flair. Guys in white aprons and tats were hot. Even hotter with bulging, flexing muscles as they joked, laughed, and threw twenty-pound salmons around as if they were as light as sardines.

I made my way to the flower stalls and picked out a twenty-five-dollar floral bunch in deep pinks and purples. The five-dollar bunches were decent. The ten-dollar ones nice. And the twenty-five-dollar bouquets were just show-offy and obscene. Like being a billionaire's wife?

I paid with the reserve cash I had in my wallet, leaving just enough for my mac and cheese. In my real life, I had to skimp. These things were luxuries. Did I want to continue to live like this? Or did I want the high life?

I felt like I was living that old story I'd had to read in school. Lady? Or the tiger? Which would I choose? And why? Write a thousand-word essay outlining your reasons for deciding to choose the billionaire. Where had that come from? Was I choosing the billionaire? And was he the equivalent of the lady or the tiger?

As I waited in line at Beecher's, being jostled and bumped by the crowds, I regretted buying flowers first. I finally got my mac and cheese and balanced it and my flowers as I made my way downstairs. The Market was always crowded. There were usually no places to sit and eat. I knew of a spot in the basement that hardly anyone bothered to find. There were generally plenty of tables there.

Sure enough, I was right. I found a table for two, set my flowers in the seat opposite me as if they were my date, and took a bite of heavenly mac and cheese. So much better than instant mac. Why did I ever bother with the pale imitation?

My phone buzzed in my purse. I ignored it. Whoever was calling could wait. A woman walked by and gawked at me as if she was trying to place me. I didn't know her, so I shrugged it off. She was probably just admiring my flowers. Then two biker dudes in full leathers and tats strolled by. It would have been a nice boost to my self-esteem to think they were checking me out.

But they wore the same *Hey, don't I know her?* expression as the woman had. Weird.

I was sitting in a low-traffic part of the Market, but the curious stares started coming faster. As the stares turned to whispers and pointing, I grew more and more uncomfortable. I wolfed downed the rest of my lunch and headed out onto the street to get my cheesecake on a stick from a walk-up window. Cheese seemed to be the food theme of my day.

As I waited in line, my phone buzzed again. And again. The more I ignored it, the crazier it went. It buzzed constantly, like an electric massager was going wild for my lipstick.

My turn finally came up. I ordered a piece of Irish cream cheesecake dipped in chocolate on a stick. I was out of cash, so I crossed my fingers and handed over my credit card to the girl behind the counter.

In the back of the shop, a TV mounted on the wall played the local noon news. The girl looked at me funny. Then glanced at my credit card and read my name before she ran it. Crap! I was in trouble now. She was going to refuse my card and I was down to my last dollar twenty in cash. It sucked being poor.

The newly insidious little thought came: *You don't have to ever be poor again.*

My phone continued buzzing. Other people were giving me strange looks. They were probably thinking, *Why doesn't she answer her stupid phone!*

Did ignoring my phone make me a crazy person? From the looks I was getting, you would think so.

The girl handed me my credit card along with my cheesecake in a white paper bag. "Kayla Lucas?" She squinted at me.

I nodded, worried that I was on their banned credit card list and I'd have to bum some change off the strangers in line around me. Move over, crazy Seattle panhandlers. Here I came.

"I thought I recognized you! You've been on the noon news." She pointed to the screen behind her, which was currently showing the weather and, therefore, not much help in making her point. It was supposed to stay sunny for the next few days, though. So, good news there. June is not the sunniest month in Seattle.

"The noon news? What?" My mouth went dry. "Why?"

My credit wasn't *that* bad. I freaked. What if the girl supposedly pretending to be me had gotten herself arrested in Reno? Didn't Johnny Cash shoot a man in Reno just to see him die? Right, that was just a song.

The girl behind the counter laughed like I was joking with her. "Congratulations on marrying Justin Green! I can't believe you snagged the city's most eligible billionaire nerd. He's not much to look at. But who cares? With all that money, he's hot. Everyone wants to be you right now. I know what I'd do if I'd just married a billionaire—call in rich!"

Crap, crap, crap! Behind me in line, the curious buzz escalated toward a celebrity-sighting fever pitch. My phone buzzed like it was about to stage a jailbreak from my purse.

"You haven't seen Justin lately. He's totally gorgeous now." I don't know why I got defensive and protected his honor. Or maybe I was protecting mine. I chided myself for being vain and shallow. Like men who forever have insisted on having beautiful girls on their arms. Did I have to have a beautiful man on mine? Was that why I was hesitating about accepting Justin's proposal?

I stuffed my dollar twenty in her tip jar on the counter, grabbed my cheesecake and credit card from her, and ran.

I didn't stop until I reached Waterfront Park and lost myself in the crowd. The marauding gulls were circling, eyeing my cheesecake. I tucked the bag under my arm. The gulls were as bad as the news media.

With trembling fingers, I pulled my phone out of my purse. I had texts and missed calls from friends, coworkers, and, most ominously, my mom.

I scanned the texts. Someone had posted my "good news" to Facebook. My page was filled with best wishes and congrats. And a few snarky comments about marrying for money. People wanted to see the ring and wedding pictures. Someone else had hashtagged and tweeted it. My mom had resorted to sending me a furious text full of threatening exclamation points, demanding I call her *now* and explain myself. Was this true? Had I married that nerdy friend of Dex's? Had he been in on it and been at the wedding? How I could I elope and not *tell* her? Was my secret wedding Pinterest board just subterfuge?

How did Mom know about my board?

I ignored all the messages and punched Justin's number with a trembling finger, trying to dial him between incoming texts, emails, and calls. When I finally got through, I crossed my fingers.

Pick up, pick up, pick up!

"Kayla?" He sounded confused, and yes, almost ridiculously pleased, that I was calling so soon.

I hated to dash his hopes.

"How can you be so calm?" I rushed my words, tripping over them as I tried to talk. "Haven't you seen the news or checked your social media accounts in the last half-hour? We're all over it! I haven't even agreed to stay married to you yet and everyone knows about our 'marriage.' *Everyone.*"

"Slow down." He sounded genuinely surprised.

My mouth had gone completely dry, and my hands shook so badly I had trouble hanging on to the phone. I took a deep breath. "Our secret lasted, like, thirty seconds. Someone just announced our marriage. *Everywhere.*"

"What?" He sounded as stunned as I felt.

"Yeah." Where had he been? A cave? I took another deep breath, trying not to hyperventilate. It was too easy to breath shallowly and quickly when I was upset. "Even my mom knows. And she's ready to kill me."

"What did you tell her?" Justin sounded worried now, too.

"Nothing. I've been ignoring her, but I can't hold her off forever. We need to talk before I call her."

"No shit," Justin said. "Where are you now? I hear gulls."

"Waterfront Park."

He swore beneath his breath. "Hang on. Stay there. I'll send a car for you. Can you meet it by Pier 59?"

"A car? No way," I said. "I'll catch the bus home and call you from there."

He cleared his throat. "Not a good idea, Kayla. People will recognize you." He paused. "And you can't go home. We need to talk first. In person. And make some decisions."

He was absolutely right. But I hesitated.

"Do you also want to be ambushed by a news crew? They'll be waiting for you, trust me." I heard him moving around. "Shit, I have to get out of here, too. I just looked out the window. There's a news crew setting up in the parking lot. Let me send the driver. I'll meet you at my place."

"Fine. Where are you now?"

"Work." He swore some more. "The board is going to be furious with me. Look, I'll have the car there as soon as I can." He paused. "Kayla?"

"Yeah?"

"Put on some sunglasses or a hat or something while you wait." Unbelievably, there was suddenly a smile in his voice.

"You want me to wear a disguise?" I shook my head. "Very funny."

"Why not? A fake mustache would be even better."

"Good idea. I'll get a pink one on a stick." I looked around like I might be spotted, and spoke so softly it was almost a whisper into the phone. "So this is what it's going to be like as your wife—a life of disguise and subterfuge? I should have just joined the CIA." I held my skirt down against the wind and clutched my flowers to me with the arm holding my phone.

"*Are* you going to be my wife?"

"I don't have much choice now, do I?" In a weird way, it was a relief to have the decision made for me. "How would we explain the real situation? Neither of us know what really happened."

"I'll take that as a yes. Not the most romantic marriage proposal acceptance in the world, but whatever," he said. He sounded happy and almost amused, damn him.

"Tell your driver to look for a girl with a huge bunch of flowers." I looked around furtively. I was not cut out to be a spy.

"All the tourists buy flowers at the market. That describes half the girls down there." Justin paused. "I'll tell him to look for the girl on the news, only with sunglasses and a pink mustache."

"Tell him my sunglasses are pink, too, and totally cute."

Fifteen excruciating minutes later, a black limo pulled up and a guy with a hand-lettered sign that said Kayla jumped out. I ran to him. He held the door open for me.

"Where are we going?" I climbed in and laid my flowers on the seat next to me. My phone had stopped buzzing, but only because I'd turned it off.

"Mr. Green's."

I stared at him, realizing I'd phrased the question wrong. "But where is that?"

He looked puzzled as he stared back at me, and I realized I'd made my first mistake. A new bride should probably know where her husband lived. In fact, she should probably be living there with him already. That was traditional, anyway.

There was an awkward moment of silence until the driver broke down and spoke. "Bellevue."

Bellevue was a big place. I stopped myself from asking for specifics and nodded as he closed the door.

We took 520 across the lake as I tried to imagine what kind of a place Justin lived in. House on the water? In a neighborhood? Half an hour later, we cruised into downtown Bellevue and pulled up in front of one of its finest skyscrapers. A news crew was camped outside.

I was hit with a wave of panic—I had no idea even which floor Justin lived on.

The driver mistook my worried expression for fear of the news crew. "Don't worry, miss. We'll get you safely to the penthouse. Stay here. I'll phone for help." He texted someone.

A minute later, a security guard appeared and elbowed his way through the crowed. As the guard opened my door, the driver wished me luck.

And then I was out in the middle of a mob of reporters shouting questions at me and snapping pictures. Until half an hour ago, Justin had been the most eligible nerd in Seattle. Notoriously private about his personal life. A workaholic who was seldom seen with a girl on his arm. Justin getting married was big news.

The security guard elbowed his way through the crowd while I kept my head down. He showed me to an elevator. When the doors opened, he typed in a code and pressed the button for the penthouse. "Have a good day, ma'am."

I barely had time to thank him before the doors closed and I was by myself. On the ride up, I felt totally dazed, like life had somehow pulled a fast one on me and was laughing about it.

When the doors pinged open on the top floor, the elevator opened directly into the penthouse.

Justin was waiting for me. "Welcome home, honey."

CHAPTER FIVE

Kayla

A dog bounded up to me. A Pomsky who was just the most adorable puppy I'd ever seen. She barked happily at me and jumped up on my legs. "Some watchdog you've got."

"Data! Down." Justin snapped his fingers at the dog as I set my flowers on a nearby table, leaned down, and scooped the puppy up. The dog ignored him.

I held her up and cuddled her to my face and let her lick it. "Data? What kind of name is that for such a precious puppy?" I cooed to the dog. "Boy or girl?"

"Girl." Justin had taken his jacket off and was now in a T-shirt and jeans. The T-shirt showed off a pair of sculpted biceps and broad shoulders that belonged on an Abercrombie model.

Crap, when had he gotten those? Maybe I wasn't as much of a liar as I thought. I had to tear my gaze away from his muscles and stop imagining the rest of the body beneath that T-shirt. If his abs were anything like his arms, he might actually be my type. Assuming he would treat me like crap, of course.

This is Justin, your husband of convenience, I reminded myself. Nothing about this was real. The marriage was made up, and the chemistry, or lack of, didn't matter.

Still cradling the happy puppy, I looked past Justin, staring at the penthouse. It was a total wall of windows with breathtaking views from every side—of the Olympic Mountains, the city, the Cascades to the east. It was modern and sparsely furnished in a chic, tasteful way, obviously by an interior designer. The place was unlike the Justin I remembered.

I pointed toward the street and scratched Data behind the ears. "Have you seen the mob of reporters down there?"

"Seen and breached. Come on, girl." He took the puppy from me. "I had to get through them, too."

I picked up my flowers. "You mean there isn't a secret, private entrance to this place? How disappointing."

His smile was achingly cute. Like his puppy. "Come on in and make yourself at home."

I ignored his reference to home and collapsed on a deep leather sofa with my flowers beside me. "Crap, this is where you live?"

"*We* live." He sat down next to me, his leg bouncing nervously as he scratched Data's chin. "*One* of the places. I'm still trying to get used to it, too. I only moved in a few months ago."

I looked around again, thinking, *This place is fabulously luxurious. My apartment will look like a dump after this. How will I ever go back to real life in a year?*

The space was not homey, but it made up for its lack of warmth by being breathtaking. Like living in a nest high above everything, or on an open prairie. Sitting in the middle of all those windows, I felt both exposed and like I was flying. Terrified and exhilarated at the same time. "How many places do you have?"

"Five? Six?" He frowned as if he was trying to remember. "Some are just investments."

I put my head in my hands. "We have to come clean. This isn't going to work. My family is going to kill me and I've already made a mistake that could give us away."

"What?" He looked so adorable when he was worried.

I couldn't blame him. "I asked the driver where you lived. I mean, I had no idea. Shouldn't a wife know where her husband lives? Where *she* lives?"

Justin let out a loud breath and laughed like he was letting his relief spill out. "That's nothing. Why would you know your address by heart so soon? We had a whirlwind courtship. Like, two hours after we two college friends got together for drinks and discovered our undying love." He paused. "Anyway, you won't make that mistake again."

I raised my head and stared at him. "Until you send me to one of your other five or possibly six homes. Maybe it's even seven."

He laughed again. "I'll write them down for you."

The living area was one open space with a kitchen on one end. Justin nodded to it. "Can I get you something? I'm well stocked. I have everything."

"A new life. Can you get me that?" I leaned my head back against the leather that was as soft as warm butter. "We need to talk. And fast. Before my parents disown me."

Data yipped like she agreed. I was going to have to rename the dog.

"No problem if they do. I'll buy you some new ones." He winked and plopped onto the sofa next to me so close that our thighs and arms brushed. Husband close. His biceps were every bit as hard as they looked as they brushed my arm and Data licked it. His thighs were pretty solid, too. I had to restrain myself from resting my hand on them. What had gotten into me? Rebound syndrome. Had to be.

I studied him, thinking his face might be cute beneath that pile of hair he called a beard. That maybe I hadn't lied to the girl at the cheesecake window about that, either. I hoped he was cute, because his body was hot. And I was fighting my reaction to it. "Justin, I didn't bargain for this. I think we should come clean—"

He set the puppy on the floor, grabbed my hand in his warm, strong one, and squeezed. I was surprised by how comforting it felt. "Look. I'm sorry your hand was forced. When I find out who leaked this, I'll make their life hell. You can still back out. I'll understand."

Yeah, but what kind of a bitch would that make me? I shook my head and pulled the marriage contract from my tote bag. "Do you have a pen?"

"What?"

"Never mind." I dug in my bag for one. "Ah, here it is. I think it's one I actually pilfered from your lawyer's office." I whipped it out and slapped the papers on the coffee table.

"Kay, you don't have to—"

I studied him. He was dead serious. Kind. Considerate. With a little fixing up...

Okay I was still being shallow. But as I stared at him, I saw a flicker of potential. I saw a project. A fixer upper. A way to help him. Beautiful exteriors weren't all they were cracked up to be. Take Eric, for example. But a bit of sex appeal was no small thing to take for granted, either. And I could give it to him. I knew I could. And then there was that fact that I was not hanging out with that squirrel on his face that he called a beard. Not. Doing. It.

"I have a condition." The words were out before I even thought about them.

His Adam's apple bobbed. He stared at me. "Sorry to hear it. I didn't know you were ill."

I'd forgotten just what a smartass Justin was. He was, after all, my cousin's good friend. "Not that kind of condition, wiseass. A stipulation before I sign. If we're going to sell this, you're going to have to look the part of my husband. You're going to have to let me make you over."

He paled. I swore he paled. Though it was hard to tell beneath all that hair. There could have been a decent-looking human being lurking in the depths. There could equally have been a weak chin. I didn't remember Justin having a cut-glass-square jaw. But I didn't remember any weakness of chin, either.

I set the pen down.

"I don't give a damn about how I look. Why would I change?"

I slid my jacket off and unbuttoned one, two, three buttons of my blouse, peeling it back to reveal my cleavage. "Is it hot in here? It feels hot to me."

I slid closer to him, flirting, making him uncomfortable. Giving him a peek at the tops of my breasts. Shameless, over-the-top flirting. "Because you supposedly love me. Truly. Madly. Deeply. And you will do anything for me. Anything. Is losing the beard a deal breaker?" I had to see how invested he was.

"No." He swallowed. Hard. "But I keep the beard."

I shook my head and ran my fingernail gently down his arm. "The beard goes or the deal's off."

"You'd turn down ten million dollars over a beard?"

I leaned into him and whispered in his ear with a gust of breath meant to tantalize him. To feel as if I was blowing in his ear. "Yes. You have to meet me halfway. I could turn it around—you'd turn down the chance to save your business over a stupid beard that you could grow back in a year?"

"I'll trim the beard," he said.

"Oh, you think you have negotiating power now, do you?" I laughed. "I'm not marrying a mountain man. Why don't we start with this? I trim the beard and we keep the dialogue open."

"Done."

I picked the pen up and signed the papers with a flourish, flashing a seductive look at Justin when I was done. "I hope I signed and initialed all the right places. If not, Harry can point them out to me tomorrow."

"He's good at that." He was staring at me with those intense brown eyes of his. They were just regular brown, deep brown. But nicely shaped and shining with an intriguing mix of intelligence and desire.

I couldn't help myself. I smiled at him. "Epic prank?"

"And grand adventure. Smart decision." He nodded toward the paperwork. "Being my wife qualifies you to eat at the best restaurants. Buy the most expensive clothes and shit. Get yourself some jewelry. Hang out at charity events and meet the movers and shakers of the city. Build connections."

"Sounds like I'm eligible if someone ever makes *Real Housewives of Puget Sound*." I paused. "I'm not sure I want any of that. I like my life."

What was I saying? My life was pretty much crap.

"I mean, I like that part of my life that's out of the public eye."

He stared at me, holding my gaze, as he put his arm on the back of the sofa, almost, but not quite, around me. Like a teenage guy making a move at the movie theater. "I probably should have hammered this point

home before you signed. But I'm a hardened business-
man used to getting what he wants. We'll have to make
this look real."

He was obviously teasing.

I put on my business expression, too. And buttoned
a button. "Of course."

He paused. "And I have staff. Who are very efficient
and professional. Exceptionally nice. And who talk."

I ruined my narrow-eyed business glare by looking
around and laughing. "Imaginary servants?"

"I gave Magda, my housekeeper and cook, and Ada,
the part-time maid, the afternoon off so we could have
some privacy," he said. "Ophelia, my personal assistant,
is on the job right now awaiting my orders and doing
damage control. She's usually here during the day if I
am."

Arranging for our privacy was smart of him. Not to
mention necessary.

"And they won't question why I wasn't here the past
couple of nights? Or why we weren't off on a fabulous
honeymoon?"

"Not a problem. If we tell them anything at all, we
tell them the truth—you had food poisoning and wanted to spend the first few nights at your place. You were
more comfortable there until you recovered. And that
explains the lack of honeymoon, too."

I studied him. "Do you have an answer for everything?"

"I try."

I scrunched my nose, thinking and back in business
mode. "I guess that same excuse might hold water for

Carl, my building manager. Though he's going to be curious about why I was served and for what."

"Your private business is none of his."

Data ran to her dog bed and came back with a rope-knot toy. She held it up for Justin to grab and play tug-o-war with her. Tug-o-war, that was exactly how I felt, like I was being tugged in two directions.

"You're right," I said.

This new Justin had more confidence than the old, young one. He took the rope and gently tugged while the adorable little thing growled and pulled, its tiny teeth sunk into the rope knot.

I studied Justin as he played with the dog, a look of total joy and affection on his face. To be honest, I felt a little jealous. Shouldn't a new bridegroom feel at least as much love for his new bride as his dog? Never mind. It didn't matter.

"No offense, but you are *so* not my type, Justin."

"You mean I have a brain." He looked up from the playfully growling puppy. "I'm not a dumbass jock?" His eyes were dancing and he looked stupidly hopeful.

Or maybe that was just my romantic imagination. "Yeah, that." I ran my gaze up and down him. "I like my men stupid and pretty."

"I'm not pretty?" He spoke to the dog. "She doesn't think I'm pretty. But you do, don't you, girl? You love all this hair on my face."

"It probably reminds her of her mother."

"Ouch," he said, glancing up at me.

I was merciless. "You walked into that one."

"Do I get points for having a good personality? Or am I short on that, too?" He was teasing. But he sounded almost hurt.

"Intelligence is sexy, Jus. If used properly. But don't discount physical chemistry. You could do better, looks-wise. Your sense of fashion is horrible. It's almost like you're trying to make yourself less attractive. You have no idea how to dress to play to your strengths. For a guy who owns an online retailer known for being chic—"

"I'm just the programmer," he said. "I dress like one. This"—he motioned to his clothes—"is my uniform. The people at Flashionista keep me pretty much out of sight. Riggins is the face of the company and handles operations."

"That's not smart business, Justin. You want to be the frontman, too." I didn't let him off the hook. "Do you ever wear *anything* other than old T-shirts and jeans?"

"I add a jacket when I need to get dressed up for something serious, like a possible divorce, or to impress someone." He winked. "We'll have to work a little harder to sell things." It was almost like he was talking to himself as he thought out loud. "You'll have to move in immediately. I'll give you a drawer."

I raised one eyebrow and looked at him like he was raving crazy. "I'll need more than *one*. A *ton* more than one."

He grinned, and I realized he'd been teasing me again.

I wasn't done negotiating. If I was going to tear up my life, I was going for minimal damage. "I keep my apartment."

Justin had stopped playing with her. The dog barked to get his attention.

He leaned down and petted her. "Absolutely. You can keep all your old life."

"Even my last name?" I studied his bent head intently, watching for any sign of weakness. "There isn't much point in changing it for a short-term marriage."

"Keep it," he said, almost too quickly. "We'll say it's for professional purposes. So you can maintain your own identity separate from my dazzling billionaire persona that could easily overwhelm it."

I rolled my eyes. But there was just enough truth to his statement. "And I like my men humble, too."

"Not from what I've seen." He looked up from the dog and arched an eyebrow. "Eric, humble? Really?"

"Shut up." I leaned down and petted Data. "He has his humble moments." I bit my lip as I did a little thinking of my own. I actually couldn't remember a single second when Eric had shown any humility at all. I changed the subject. "You'll have to meet my parents *and* friends."

He shrugged again.

"No, you don't *get* it. Like, you'll really have to fool them. Head-on, headlong, award-winning performance of your life to sell this whirlwind romance. To my entire set of friends and whole family. Some members of my family have IQs as high as yours." The thought of him convincing my family made me tingle with anxiety.

"You mean your cousin Dex?" He shook his head like he was unimpressed.

"And my uncle and aunt, and Mom and Dad. And my best friend Brittany has more emotional intelligence than you have IQ points. She can smell an emotional fake from across the city. She's probably already sniffed us out as pretenders. You'll have to fool her.

"You should be scared. Very, very scared. Neither group will be easy to pull the wool over. My parents will expect responsibility and common goals. That kind of crap. My friends will expect tons of affection and passion between us. Like hands-all-over passion. Anything short of that fails their smell test."

"Okay." He agreed too readily, but his face was a mask.

I squinted at him, unable to figure him out. Was he into me or not? Cocky or just scared? "How did it happen?"

"What?"

"The wedding." I scooped up the puppy and held her in my lap so I could get his full attention. Cute baby animals were such attention grabbers. "Before I call everyone I need to know *all* the details—what I wore, where it was held, the flowers. Was there cake? Who stood up for us?"

Data sank down in my lap and kneaded my thighs with her tiny paws as I petted and cooed to her.

"How the hell do I know any of this?" he said, his tone indifferent. As if the details didn't matter and were of no interest to anyone. "I was blacked out, apparently."

"And yet this marriage is somehow legal."

Data rested her head on her paws and yawned.

"I put a PI on it after you left me in the middle of our wedding night."

"*I* didn't leave you. Just remember that." It seemed important he understood that. I still got the feeling he didn't believe that I hadn't married him. "What did the PI find out? Are there any pictures?"

Justin shook his head and looked ruefully at the dog. "They say we came in slightly bombed."

I arched an eyebrow. "Slightly? Seriously?"

"Totally shitfaced."

I laughed. "That's better. It doesn't sound like me, but that's better. And?"

"We bought the cheapest wedding package. Refused to have our picture taken, even when the paid witness offered to snap one on our phones. And strolled, or maybe staggered, out of the chapel, laughing all the way."

"Nice."

"And they think you wore a pink dress."

"Thank God for that," I said. "At least I look good in pink." I had another moment of panic. "What about the ring? What did you use for a ring? Should I have it?"

He looked a little sheepish. "According to the highly reliable witness, I used my Order of the Engineer ring."

I gave him a puzzled look and my heart stopped. I had no idea what an order of the engineer ring was. Part of me didn't want to know. If it was customized like a class ring, we were sunk. "Is it distinctive? That could be a problem—"

He shook his head. "No. It's a plain stainless steel ring. There's no way to identify it as mine." He held up his right hand and wiggled his baby finger where a totally plain, thin stainless steel band glinted unimpressively in the light. "Like this one. We wear them on our baby fingers."

"You got another one already?"

"I ordered an extra before the initiation ceremony," he said. "I have a habit of losing rings."

I held my ring-empty hand out to him like a princess giving her hand to a knight for a kiss. "Hand it over and slip it on me."

He took my hand and reluctantly slid the ring off his finger. Then, it may have been my imagination, but his hand trembled as he slipped his ring on my left ring finger.

"It fits perfectly." I was surprised and let it show. As I tried to pull my hand from his, he bent and kissed my ring finger. His mouth was warm and his touch surprisingly tender—surprising period. My heart raced as his mouth met my fingers and his beard tickled my skin.

"My hand feels empty without that ring." How did he make that simple statement sound so romantic? As if he'd given his prize possession to me.

The dog shifted in my lap. "We'll order you another one."

I held my hand up to admire my new piece of jewelry, if you could call it that, and suppressed a frown. For an improvised ring, it wasn't bad. Better than a cigar band. Or a rubber band. For a wedding ring from a billionaire, it pretty much sucked big time. "The bigger problem is that we'll have to hope no one noticed you wearing this one for the last few days."

"People are surprisingly unobservant. I wouldn't worry about it. Besides, I can claim I was wearing a spare and then I lost that one." He must have seen my look of disappointment, even though I'd tried to hide it. "We'll get you another one, a real wedding ring."

"This one's fine." I put my hand down and tucked it under my legs.

"No, it isn't." His voice was tender and firm at the same time. "You're obviously my trophy wife. You need a trophy ring."

"Jus, you do realize you married an older woman? Aren't trophy wives usually younger?" I had to be three or four years older than he was. "How old are you, anyway?" I hadn't thought about his age until now.

"Twenty-one."

Crap, I was a cradle robber. A cougar at nearly twenty-five. "A baby." I leaned in to whisper to him again in my flirty voice. "At least you're drinking age."

"Is that an insult?"

"Maybe."

"Statistically, it's smart of you to marry a younger man. Less chance of being a widow."

I shrugged. "Of course you have a smart wife. A brilliant wife. Top of my class, so you know. And no wisecracks about my choice of degree. But it doesn't matter. We'll be divorced long before our twilight years and lifespan statistics catch up to us." I twisted the cheap ring on my finger. "I'll give this fine piece of jewelry back...when this is over. Back to our story. The details?"

He got that embarrassed look again. "I was drinking alone, and pretty hammered already, when you approached me at the bar. I bought you a drink, and then another. We drank until we were both plastered. Then one of us, I think it was you, thought we should be spontaneous and do something crazy."

"No." I shook my head vehemently.

His brow furrowed. "What? That's what the PI pieced together. As I say, I don't remember a thing past getting smashed at the bar. You think you wouldn't ask me to marry you? I'm a billionaire. Everyone wants me."

"No. Yeah. Whatever. I would *not* ask you to marry me, billionaire or not. When I get married—"

"You are married."

I ignored him. "—for real, I will expect the guy to do the proposing. In some *romantic* way." I paused for effect. "We have another problem."

"What?" He looked genuinely worried that I'd come up with a deal breaker. Even though I'd just signed the deal. "Everyone knows I would never elope. I've been planning my wedding since I was five. Maybe before. I even have a secret Pinterest board where I pin my latest preferences and ideas."

He held my gaze and his voice went soft. "People do crazy stuff when they're in love." It was almost as if he was talking about himself.

I ignored it. He was probably toying with me. I motioned between the two of us. "Like you and me?"

He nodded. "And marrying a billionaire? Who insisted on getting married right away? Who could resist that?"

I rolled my eyes, but I was smiling at him. "You're incorrigible. But I guess we'll have to run with it. What about your friends and family? How hard will they be to convince?"

He shrugged. "My friends will high-five me. My brothers will give me crap. And Mom and Dad will be suspicious that you married me for my money. And possibly hostile about it." His self-deprecating humor was sweet, but there was an edge to it.

"And they'd be right. Kind of." I scrunched my mouth to one side, like I did when I was unhappy and trying to deal with it. "We'll deal with that later if we have to. Will they want to meet me?"

"Sure. When we're all in town."

"They won't be surprised and eager to meet the girl who stole their little boy's heart?"

"I'm no one's 'little' boy and never have been." His voice was hard. "I do what I want. When I want. And don't give a damn what people think. They're used to my eccentricities."

I frowned, not sure I believed him. But he believed what he was saying. That much was clear. "The good news is I won't really *have* to impress them. If they don't like me, it will be that much easier for them when we get divorced next year."

He winced. I swore he did.

I took a breath. "Ring. Dress. Witnesses," I said, ticking off wedding elements. "Have we missed anything I need to know? Flowers?"

"Roses. Red."

"Almost like a poem. Good. Though not terribly creative. Vows?"

"Standard, I think."

"Did I promise to...love you...through sickness and health?" Why had I stumbled on the word *love?*

"I assume so."

"Wedding night?"

He gave me a deadpan stare. "Your parents are going to ask about that? Are they going to want to see the sheets and make sure you were a virgin, too?"

I gave him a gentle shove. "Virgin! Ha ha. I meant, what hotel were we in? Did we have the honeymoon suite?"

"Same hotel we both were staying in for business. We went back to my room." He looked almost apologetic. "It was a suite, at least."

I shook my head. "This is going to be a hard sell. Ready to have some fun? Let's call my parents!"

CHAPTER SIX

Justin

Next to me, Kayla pulled her phone from her purse without disturbing the puppy. I realized with a jolt that I was outnumbered by females. In my own home. And I'd brought it on myself. Data was curled cozily in Kayla's lap. I'd signed myself up for a bargain with the devil. If this scheme failed, I was in danger of losing the dog *to* the girl at the end of the year.

Kayla turned her heart-melting, yet beautifully devious, smile on me. She was like Eve tempting me to eat the apple. "The minute I turn this thing on, all hell is going to break loose again."

I couldn't disagree. "Nonstop calls. Texts with a dozen exclamation points. Curious friends and family. Worried parents. Bring them on."

After the last three years getting Flashionista off the ground, anything else was child's play. Even calling her parents and lying my ass off.

My phone was off, too. I hadn't turned it off since I'd started Flashionista with Riggins. This was serious shit for me.

"A fearless man?" Kayla arched one eyebrow. "A hero. I like it." She grabbed my arm. Damn, I was too aware of her touch as she stared seriously into my eyes. "Let *me* do the talking."

She laughed. "I'm an adult. Totally self-sufficient and off on my own. Why do I feel like I'm back in kindergarten about to be scolded for pinching a boy and ending up in the principal's office?" She bumped me playfully with her shoulder. I prickled with awareness of her. "I'm going to put it on speakerphone. If they know you can hear them, they'll behave themselves."

She grinned devilishly as she hit the on button. "Once Mom picks up, prepare to be yelled at. In the highest-pitched voice human ears can hear. Mom perfected the art of screeching. But she's basically harmless. It means she's worried, that's all." She took a deep breath. "Here goes."

"Kayla Marie Lucas! At last. *Thank goodness.*" The relief in her mom's voice was palpable. And shrill.

"Hey, Mom!" Kayla winked at me and mouthed, *Told you so.* She smiled as if her mom's reaction amused her. As if it were the most natural thing in the world. "Is Daddy around? I have some news."

Daddy? I mouthed back, unable to decide if that was sweet or needy. Or purely playful. And whether I was up against an overprotective father who doted on his daddy's girl and would come after me with his shotgun. Too late for that, apparently. I'd already married her. What was he going to do? Make me un-marry her?

"Don't *Hey, Mom* me. And your *daddy* is not going to save you. So you can stop that blatant manipulation. No teasing. No playful horsing around. This is *serious*. He's Dad to you, thank you very much." There was the mom voice.

Kayla's kindergarten reference had been entirely appropriate. I grinned at her.

"I saw your *news* on the news," her mom said in a huff. "I want to know one thing—is it true? Did you marry that *boy*?"

Boy? I mouthed to Kayla and made a muscle, pointing to it and flexing to show her I was *not* a boy.

She squeezed my bicep like it was ripe fruit. Damn, her simple touch made me horny as hell. I was a man lost.

She made a kissy mouth at me and flashed me a thumbs-up. I was in real danger of losing control and actually kissing her. Like a dumb shit who thought her flirting was real. We were partners in crime. Two people sharing a secret. In on a gag. Coconspirators. That was all. The temptation to just do it was too strong. I blamed my family and all their damned sporting events. I had to force my gaze away from her shiny, pink, high-gloss lips as her mom rattled on.

"I told your dad—seriously, Kayla, he's on my side on this one—I told him this must be one of those ridiculous tabloid stories run amok, the ones that are pure fiction. Totally made up because the facts don't matter. Just the sensation it makes."

I was feeling a lot of sensations, too.

Her mom's sigh was heavy. "Probably a slow news day in the city. Our beautiful, romantic girl marrying that nerdy friend of Dex's? Simply ridiculous! Why would you? You're no mercenary bitch. You'd never marry a man *just* for his money. There would have to be *more* to it. And what other reason could there possibly be with a friend of Dex's?"

I held my hands out, pointed to myself, and raised my eyebrows, like *What* is *she talking about? Look at this hot hunk of manhood?*

Kayla put a hand over her mouth to keep from laughing.

"I love that boy. Dex is like a son to me. But...his friends? Not exactly heartthrobs, are they? I told your dad it makes no sense. Unless our crazy nephew is pranking us all again. I can see Dex doing something like this, calling in a bogus news story for the fun of it. Because he's bored."

"I reminded your dad you had food poisoning over the weekend. Remember? You called us sick as a dog from Reno. All upset your boss was going to fire you. We had to talk you down from that tree." She sighed into the phone again. "That damned Eric! I blame him. I could throttle that boy."

For the food poisoning? Her thoughts were random and her argument incoherent. But at least Eric was a boy in her opinion, too. I didn't feel so bad now. I was in good company?

"I'm sick to death of the rollercoaster he's put you on since you met him. You're up. You're down—"

"Mom. The news story is true. I married Justin." Some of the enthusiasm and amusement left Kayla's voice. As if she had regained the sense of gravity over what she'd done.

My heart pounded. I was as nervous as a real prospective bridegroom asking for a daughter's hand.

On the other end of the phone, her mom gasped dramatically. "No! I'm warning you, if you're pranking me, too, I'm cutting you out of our will and leaving everything to charity." Her mom laughed, nervously. Hopefully. As if she wanted to believe Kayla was in on the joke.

At least she wasn't drooling over my money.

"Sorry, Mom. I did. I eloped with him in Reno." Kayla glanced at me and sighed.

"No! No, no, no, *no*! You didn't. You did not. I don't believe you. Eloping? This is so not like you, the girl who's been planning her dream wedding since she was in the womb."

She paused as if she was trying to compose herself. "How could you? Your dad and I had first right of refusal on all future sons-in-law." Her voice caught. She sounded as if she was trying not to cry. As if she was fighting to be reasonable. "Whatever possessed you to marry a billionaire on the rebound? Eric is *not* worth throwing your life away over."

Throwing her life away over? We were off to a good start. Obviously, I wasn't their first choice for a son-in-law. I looked at Kayla. At the mention of Eric, she'd looked away and gotten tears in her eyes. Damn him.

Whatever anyone thought, I was *not* worse than Eric. At least marriage to me wasn't a life sentence with a cheating idiot.

"I'm sorry, Mom. It happened so fast." She glanced at me and winked. "I didn't marry Justin out of spite. You have to believe me. That's the absolute truth."

"Why *did* you marry him?" her mom said.

A male voice came on the line. "It's all right, Debbie. Give it a rest. Let the girl explain. We'll sort this out. What's going on, Lala?"

Lala? I mouthed to Kayla, trying to cheer her up and lighten the mood. I was instantly in love with her nickname.

Long story, she mouthed back. "Hey, Daddy!"

"Our daughter married a geeky friend of Dex's," Debbie said. "I don't believe you didn't do it to get back at Eric, Kayla. Why else would you—" Her mom muttered something to herself. "That's not something else you want to tell us before the news does, is there?"

Kayla looked like she was trying not to laugh. "I'm not pregnant, if that's what you mean."

"Thank goodness for that!" Her mom's sigh of relief could have been heard in Kansas.

So she wasn't looking forward to geeky grandbabies fathered by me, either.

"Why can't you just accept that I'm a grown woman, Mom?" Kayla said. "This is my life. I can marry whom I like. And I wanted to marry Justin. I don't have to explain my reasons. I don't even have to have any reasons." She paused and smiled at me, as if this was a grand joke. "I love him, Mom."

My heart tripped over itself, even though I knew she was lying. I would have to watch my new wife. She was a cool liar.

"Love him?" Her mom scoffed. "How could you love him? Love takes time to grow. You don't even *know* him. You haven't mentioned him in years. If only you'd called us, we would have talked sense into you and stopped you." Her mom couldn't stop lamenting the loss.

Kayla looked away. "Justin is sitting next to me. He can hear everything you say. I probably should have mentioned that upfront." She laughed lightly, as if she was trying to relieve the tension. "He'd like to talk to you."

Debbie went silent immediately. Kayla mouthed, *Secret weapon* to me and held her phone between us with her head bent over it. She held it up closer to my lips and whispered, "Say something. This is your chance. Impress them."

Our foreheads nearly brushed. I wanted to kiss her so badly it hurt. She shot me an encouraging smile. In her lap, Data made a happy puppy snort.

What does a guy say in a situation like this? My mouth went dry at the thought of reality. I cleared my throat, nervous as hell. I hadn't been this anxious since I was selling the value of Flashionista to our initial investors. Very little made me jittery any more.

"Mrs. Lucas. Mr. Lucas. This...this...beautiful thing took us by surprise, too. I know it seems quick and sudden to you. I hear your doubts about Kayla being on the rebound. If I were a parent, I'd probably have the same concerns.

"But you haven't seen us together. Seen how much we love each other. I *love*, Kayla. I love your daughter.

"Do you believe in love at first sight? I do. I fell in love with her the moment she walked into my class in college. From the minute I laid eyes on her.

"I don't have to date her for years to know she's the girl for me. I've learned in business, sometimes you feel it in your gut when something is right and meant to be. You have to seize the moment before it passes you by. I'm going to treat your daughter right and do everything in my power to make her happy. I'll be a good husband to her. I give you my word."

I glanced at Kayla. She didn't meet my eye.

"Look on the bright side," I said into the silent phone. "I may not be much to look at, but I have boatloads of money. I can definitely afford a wife. Even one who likes to shop."

Kayla bumped me with her shoulder and mouthed, *Shut up.* I winked at her.

Her dad laughed. "Kayla does like to shop."

"We have as good a shot as any couple." I was lying through my teeth. The odds of my success were abysmal.

There was a moment of stunned silence where no one seemed to know what to say. I prided myself on my debating skills. I'd made a convincing case. From the look on Kayla's face, I knew I had.

"Dad? Mom?" Kayla shrugged, like *What's going on?*

"Yeah?" Debbie's voice was softer and calmer now.

"We were going to tell you," Kayla said. "But we wanted to do it in person. Somehow the news leaked to the media and they beat us to it. And, for the record, I really did have food poisoning."

"I'll bet that made for an interesting wedding night," my new father-in-law said. "If a marriage can survive the complete lack of romance and mystery of puking, maybe you stand a chance, after all."

Now *there* was a vote of confidence.

Her mom still wasn't buying it. "Nice try, Kayla. But when you elope, it's common courtesy to call your parents. If you tell me you're already having second thoughts and are thinking about getting divorced after four days—" The words were harsh, but Debbie's tone was soft and almost confused. It was like she had rehearsed a speech and was plowing ahead with it when she'd already lost confidence with the message, but didn't know what else to say.

"No, Mom." Kayla glanced at me guiltily. "We're not getting divorced."

I shouldn't have done it, but I caught Kayla's free hand in mine and squeezed it.

"We'll have to throw a reception," her mom said, as if that settled things. "As soon as possible. People will expect a reception. And, of course, we want to meet Justin."

"You've met him before, Mom."

"You know what I mean. As someone special. A member of the family." Debbie's voice trembled. "We want to see this great love for ourselves. Come for dinner. When's good? How about tonight? I can throw something together in a jiffy."

Kayla glanced at me for confirmation as I pulled up my calendar and made a show of looking at it. I knew full well I had a commitment. "Can't tonight. Sorry. Meeting I can't miss."

"You can't get out of it?" She pouted prettily.

I shook my head. "Afraid not." It was unfortunate timing, but I'd been looking forward to this for a while. I couldn't bail. I tried to look apologetic.

What the hell? Kayla shot me a look of relief. "Not tonight, Mom."

Her mom sighed. "That's too bad. I suppose billionaires are busy people." She sounded ticked off. "And Wednesday's out. We have a dinner that night *we* can't get out of."

I didn't know. Was she trying to one up me? Show me that they were busy, important people, too? She'd always seemed pleasant enough the few times I'd met her.

Kayla eyed me. "Thursday?"

I nodded and gave her a thumbs-up.

"Thursday is no good. Bunko," Debbie said. "If I miss it this time, the girls will fillet me. Friday?"

Kayla looked to me again. "Justin?"

I nodded.

"Friday works," Kayla said to her mom.

Just then Data woke up and barked happily.

"Is that a dog?" Debbie asked.

Kayla scratched Data behind her ears. "Yep. Justin's."

"It sounds like a *small* dog." Debbie's voice dripped accusation. The way she said it was almost an affront to my masculinity.

"It's a Pomsky!" Kayla's eyes lit up, like this was a most wonderful thing.

I loved her excitement about it.

"Oh, heavens!" Debbie didn't sound happy. "A Pomsky! You've *always* wanted one." She muttered something about underhanded dealings and tempting her daughter with a dog.

As if my billions had been nothing at all. Or my lovable, hot self. But the dog, she was the instrument of all temptation.

"She's incredibly cute," Kayla cooed to the dog, the way I wished she would coo to me, while she stroked Data's chin. "You'll love her. She's small, even for a Pomsky. Completely huggable. I think I'll put her in a purse." She grinned at me.

"You will not put her in a purse. She's not all *that* small. She's still growing. She'll get bigger," I whispered to Kayla. "The breeder assured me she'd be on the large side. For a Pomsky." I was defensive as hell. As if my manhood had been attacked. I'd really thought she'd be bigger.

Kayla raised an eyebrow and whispered back to me, "Size issues? Really?"

"Size matters," I muttered. I didn't want her thinking I didn't, cough, have a manly dog.

"We'll see you Friday," Debbie said.

Kayla

I stared at Justin. "Impressive acting skills. Nice delivery on the professions of love. Even I almost believed them. My parents were fighting it, but I think they were a little taken in, too. Just don't overdo it. We don't want my parents loving you too much. Or things to have to go too sour in a year. We want an amicable divorce. That was the agreement.

"The less explaining we have to do then, the better. If a man loved me as much as you just professed to, why would I ever leave you? See my point?"

His face was a mask. "Sorry. I got caught up in the moment. I'm used to saying what I have to in order to get what I want. You learn a thing or two from running a business—mainly, tell your clients what they want to hear."

"You mean lie?" I pointed at him.

"Lie? Everything I said was the truth—I will be a good husband to you. For as long as we last."

I tilted my head and shook it. "And all that about love?"

He looked uncomfortable. "Just a stretch of the truth. My gut said to do this fake marriage."

"Whatever you say. But now that I've seen what a smooth liar you are, I'm not going to trust a thing that you say." I gave him a playful punch in the arm and hit rock-solid muscle.

Just then my phone buzzed in my hand. I glanced at the screen. "It's Britt! She's trying to FaceTime me.

You remember Britt? My best friend? I have to get this. Just stay out of the picture." I handed him the dog and slid to the far side of the sofa away from him. I picked up the call with a smile plastered on my face.

Britt's face smiled back at me. "About time!" Excitement made her even more animated than usual. "How could you run off and get married without me! I can't believe you broke the deal we made when we were freshman. In high school. You remember the one— maids of honor at each other's weddings."

I grimaced. Guilty as charged. "Yeah, I know. Sorry. That was crappy of me. Things moved"—I slid a sideways look at Justin—"too fast to get you there in time. If it's any consolation, I missed you!"

"I certainly hope so! We didn't even get to do a wedding Pinterest board together." Britt studied me, looking like she was trying to figure out what to say. "Did you *really* marry geeky Justin Green?" She sounded more concerned than judgmental.

Beside me, Justin pointed to himself and whispered, "I'm right here. Let her know I'm here."

Out of view of the camera, I made a cutting motion, meaning for him to shut up.

"I knew you were upset about Eric moving in with Jessica. I can see how you'd want to spite him. But, Kay, you've dated some *really* hot guys. Including Eric. He was a douche, but he was still hot. Money aside, Justin Green? Really? That just doesn't seem like you. He's not your type." Her brow furrowed, like she was worried about me. "Do you love him?" She sounded as if she couldn't believe I did.

Justin slid up behind me and tried to get into the picture. I blocked him and scooted so he was out of the frame. I had to convince Britt that this sham marriage was what I wanted. Which wasn't easy. I hated lying to her.

"Of course I do!" In a platonic way. "He's..." I glanced at him again, trying to come up with some good points.

He looked too hopeful as he waited for me to rattle off his many wonderful attributes like a happy, besotted bride should. But I was still drawing a blank. He made that rolling motion with his hand that meant, *Get on with it.*

"He's hotter than he looked, Britt."

That got Justin to back off. He pulled back and grinned at me when I gave him a sidelong look. Then he did that peacock guy thing of making a muscle again.

"Hotter than he looks?" Britt's furrow deepened. "What is that supposed to mean? I was expecting something...a little less superficial."

I blushed and my heart raced. Sweet Britt. She always wanted the best for me. "Looked. Hotter than he *looked.* It means he's gotten hotter since college."

"Or you've gotten more desperate."

"He's definitely gotten hotter. You wouldn't recognize him now." Damn, I was going to have to work a makeover miracle now.

Justin tried to angle his way into the picture again. "Give her a chance to see my hotness." He tried to peek around my shoulder. When I wouldn't let him, he lifted the hair on the back of my neck and nuzzled his bearded face into it, tickling me.

I laughed involuntarily and scrunched my shoulders to fend him off. At the same time, my skin prickled with awareness of him.

"Is he there?" Britt gave me a dark look. "Why didn't you tell me?"

"Sorry. He's not *supposed* to be here." I glared at him and pushed him away.

He laughed in response.

"I heard that laughter. Put him on!" Britt pointed into the phone. "I want to see this hotter-than-he-looked billionaire husband of yours."

"He can't come to the phone right now."

"He's indisposed, is he? He's sitting right behind you. I got a glimpse of the top of his head."

"He can't come to the phone," I repeated.

She gave me her piercing, thin eyes. "Is he naked? Did I interrupt something?" She gave me a knowing, lewd look.

I sighed. "He's not naked. He's busy minding his own business." I brushed him away with my hand.

"He'd better not be too busy to meet me and the rest of the gang. Soon." She pointed into the phone again. "Hear that, Justin? I know you're listening. Put me on the calendar."

"And you." She pointed directly at me. "I'm going to get all the down and dirty details. When he isn't listening in." She laughed and glanced to the side suddenly. "Oh, crap! Here comes my boss. Gotta run. See you two glowing newlyweds soon. Newlyweds! That's so crazy." She shook her head and she was gone.

I turned and made thin eyes at Justin, imitating Britt. "What was that about? I told you to let me handle this."

"Henpecked already?" But he was grinning. "I did so well with your parents, I thought I'd help out with your friends." His eyes danced.

I couldn't help smiling. "You're enjoying this *way* too much. You must not get out much."

"A guy *should* enjoy his honeymoon."

I shook my head and laughed. "Honeymoon! Is that what this is?" Then I had a pang of anxiety. "Everyone will expect a honeymoon. Why aren't we on one?"

"Had to be postponed until after the latest bushfire with Flashionista."

"You have an answer for everything."

"This one's the truth. One thing you'll learn about me, Kayla. I'm a workaholic."

"So that's why you haven't found anyone to spend your money on before." I smiled back at him and assessed him. Could I really make him hot?

"Uh-oh!" he said.

"What?"

"You're biting your lip. You only bite your lip when you're thinking up some kind of trouble." He took a breath. "You did in college, anyway."

"The things you notice about me are so sweet." I studied him some more and reached out and stroked his beard. "Huh. Surprisingly soft."

"Does that mean I get to keep it?"

"Not a chance." I took a deep breath. "Grab your phone. Your parents are up next."

He pulled his phone out of his pocket, turned it on, and began typing, his thumbs flying.

"What are you doing?" I tried to peek at his phone.

"Telling my parents."

"You're texting them?" I couldn't believe him. "You can't text them news like this." I reached for his phone.

He was too quick. And I was too late. Damn those flying thumbs.

He hit send before I could stop him. "Done." His winning grin was cute, though.

His phone buzzed almost instantly. "Incoming! See? No problem. They're thrilled."

"Or royally angry."

He read the messages silently and smiled at me. "They're both out of the country on business. But even given the time zone differences, they responded immediately. Like I said. They're thrilled. They've heard the news. They appreciate me confirming the validity of the stories. And they send their congrats. They'll see us at the earliest convenience when they're both back in town."

"When will that be?"

He shrugged. "They're not around much. If we manage things right, we could conceivably go the entire year avoiding them." He grinned.

"You're evil."

"Only when I want to be."

"And now I see where you get your stunning social skills."

He looked a bit crestfallen.

"Sorry," I said. "That was mean. Every family has their own behavioral standards. Yours are just a bit...different from most people's." I took a deep breath. "Well, that went well, then, right?"

"It's pretty typical for them. They're used to me going my own way and doing what I want. They haven't been able to stop me since I was about two. We're grown people, Kay. We don't need our parents' approval."

"True," I said. "But I love my family. It makes life easier if they're happy for us."

I tapped the arm of the sofa. We had a lot to do and deal with. My com training was coming out. "Now that we've told our parents, we need to issue an official statement to get the press off our backs. After that, we both need to post the good news to our social media. It will look better for us if the official announcement comes first. Then my friends won't accuse me of making this up and faking it as a joke." I sighed. "This faking is exhausting."

"I don't want you worn out around me." Sweet sincerity, thy name is Justin. "Let's make a deal—you *never* fake things with me." His eyes were dark and serious.

"Never?"

"Not even once."

"May I remind you, never is a long time."

"Not an issue." He sounded too supremely confident.

Which got my hackles up. Me? Competitive? Never. Oh, wait. Never was a long time. "Not even to spare your feelings? Not even orgasms?"

His eyes lit up. Why did I insist on flirting with him? He was so easy to be around and joke with. And I think I wanted to see a hint of that old spark he'd had for me in college. Maybe it was cruel of me. Maybe I was a jealous bitch for not wanting men, him, to forget me. Or maybe I was just human.

"Especially not orgasms." Damn that sexy voice of his. He was flirting back. "If we ever sleep together"— he may as well have said *when*—"you won't have to fake it."

"Braggart. That's too bad. I do a mean *When Harry Met Sally* imitation. Want me to show you?" I closed my eyes and tipped my head back. "Oh, oh, oh—"

He covered my mouth with his hand. "No thank you."

I pushed his hand away. "Too bad." I laughed. "The neighbors will be expecting to hear those kinds of noises. That and bed thumping. We're supposed to be young, horny newlyweds."

"This place is sound insulated. The neighbors can't hear us."

"Again. Too bad." I Googled "sample wedding announcement wording. Celebrities."

Justin leaned over my shoulder. "What are you doing?"

"Getting ideas for our announcement." I grimaced. "We love each other a lot so we finally tied the knot," I read aloud from a website that gave examples of wording. "Bad rhyming couplets. No." I shook my head and shuddered. "Just *no*."

"I like it." He nudged me with his shoulder. "It's cute. It's perfect. It's concise." He wiped a fake tear away. "It brings tears to the eyes."

I rolled my eyes. "It brings tears, all right. You'd better be teasing. If you aren't, I'm tearing up that document I just signed and the deal is off for lack of taste."

His answering laugh was deep and rich. Sexy the way it rolled up from deep inside him. I ignored the way the sound of it made me smile and began composing.

For Immediate Release

Billionaire entrepreneur Justin Green—

He was hanging on my shoulder, reading over it. "FYI. My middle name is...Arnold." Justin cleared his throat, obviously exaggerating his embarrassment.

"What?" I stared blankly at him.

"Are you going to make me say it again?" He sighed dramatically. "Arnold. My middle name is Arnold. Lame name, I know. I think my dad was a fan of the golfer. I was a tiny, sickly preemie. He didn't see me playing football, not even in the peewee league. He was hoping I could make it on the links." His last sentence was laced with innuendo.

What was a girl to do? I flirted back. Because it was safe and easy. And kept the tension at bay. "Can you...make it on the links?"

"I don't know. I haven't tried. We could try together."

I laughed. "That was the worst come-on in the history of come-ons."

He shrugged. "We're married now. The romance and the trying to impress is over, baby."

"That's what you think." I didn't know why I said that.

His eyes lit up.

I hadn't meant to give him false hope. "So? Can you? Golf?"

"Not well."

"Too bad. I'm pretty good, actually." I winked.

He cleared his throat and pointed to my phone, reverting to the original topic. "You saw my middle name on the marriage license. It probably just slipped your mind. People will be expecting you to know it. It's standard to put it in wedding announcements and invitations, isn't it?"

"How do you know that?" I stared at him in amazement. "Most men don't care, don't care, and don't care."

"I'm a nerd." His grin was adorably self-deprecating. And a bit heartbreaking at the same time. The guy was one of the country's richest millenials. And he self-identified as a nerd.

"This isn't a newspaper announcement," I said. "It's a press release from your office. If you don't want to list it, you don't have to put it in."

"Okay. My mistake. Leave it out. Carry on."

Billionaire entrepreneur Justin Green confirms that he eloped with his college sweetheart, and longtime love, fashion buyer Kayla Marie Lucas, over the week-

end in Reno, Nevada. The nuptials took place on Friday, June 6th in a late-night ceremony at a twenty-four-hour wedding chapel. The couple recently reunited and has kept their relationship quiet. Family members and friends were surprised by the announcement, but pleased for the happy couple.

Justin is very much in love with Kayla. He asks that you respect their privacy during this honeymoon period.

"Think that will hold them off for a year?" I asked.

Justin read over my shoulder. "College sweetheart?"

"I'm trying to lend an air of...what's the word? An air of not getting drunk and getting married without remembering a thing to a classmate you haven't seen in years. On a whim. To reassure the market and your board that you took this commitment, and huge life step, seriously. As you take everything."

"An air of relationship longevity." He nodded. "Of careful consideration. I see. I like it. But what about Eric? Anyone who knows you, us, will know I was a geek you'd never date. All any reporter has to do is ask any one of your friends, family, profs, sorority sisters, coworkers. The garbage man—"

"Shut up!" I leaned my head back to look at him. And got mostly a face full of beard, ruining the sexy effect of his voice and laugh. And wit.

"Or mine. They'll swear you were out of my league. And, I hate to point this out, you were with Eric."

"Off and on. I was with him off and on. I could have been with you at one point in the off phase. You and I studied together a lot." I held my phone up. "This is from your point of view. You could have misinterpreted that studying as dating."

"I see," he said again, with a tease in his voice. "Isn't this announcement lopsided? I'm madly in love with you, apparently. But you seem aloof. There's no mention of how much you love me." Whispered in my ear, his deep voice was like chocolate. Delicious and tempting.

"Again. This is an announcement from *you*. You're being modest. Unassuming. Sweet, professing your undying love. But I did say we're a happy couple. Now we just need to have your office send this out to the news outlets."

He put his hand on my shoulder just as his phone rang.

It startled Data awake. She barked and jumped off my lap.

Justin glanced at his phone. "It's my assistant. I have to take this." He held up a finger, indicating I should give him a moment.

I turned away to give him some privacy. But not before I saw the way his face softened when he picked up. "Ophelia." He caressed her name. His voice even went a little gooey in a deep chocolate way.

My heart pounded as I looked out the glass walls to the city around us and tried not to hear the intimate, familiar way he spoke to her. It wasn't as if I'd had a lot of time to think about things, but this was the first time I'd even considered that he'd given up his freedom, too.

He claimed there was no one else in his life. But maybe that simply meant there was no one else *at this moment.* That he hadn't had a chance to make his move. The way he was talking to Ophelia certainly sounded as if he liked her.

"Okay...sure...sounds good...yep," he murmured to her, and laughed.

My phone began buzzing, too. I got a text from Dex.

"About time," I whispered to myself. I'd been wondering when he would weigh in.

Just heard the news. Best wishes, Lala. Isn't that the socially acceptable thing to say to the bride? Here's what I really want to say: What the shit? Don't tell me you fell for his money? How the hell did he trick you into marrying him? Whatever con he pulled, it was epic.

Treat him well and give him a chance. You two could be adorable together. Your words. Ha ha.

Seriously, you could have done a lot worse. You've risen in my estimation. Your taste in men has improved, anyway. Brains over brawn, Lala. Good choice. Give the blushing groom my congrats.

Conned into marriage? I turned to stare at Justin. He was still talking animatedly to the fair Ophelia. God, what a name. Poor thing.

No, I thought. *He wouldn't. He likes her. What have I done? What have we done? Is there any chemistry between us at all? Can I actually fake this?*

He saw me staring at him and smiled, confused by the way I was looking at him. I slid next to him and covered his hand that was holding the phone.

You know, I wasn't a sharing person. Never had been. I certainly wasn't going to share my husband. Not for a year, anyway.

I pulled the phone out of his hand, hit "end," and tossed it to the other end of the sofa. He stared at me, surprised, but wordless, as I looked into his eyes. I saw myself reflected. But what I really wanted to see was how he saw me. How he felt. How I felt. There was only one way to find out.

Dex's taunting rang in my ears as clearly as if he'd spoken the words aloud. I slid into Justin's lap, facing him, perched over him in the position of power. I watched him swallow, hard. Watched his eyes cloud with confusion as I took his bearded face firmly in my hands and let my long hair envelope our faces. As my skirt flared around his jeans, I lowered my crotch against his and rocked and rubbed against him.

His breath caught as I lowered my lips to his and gently pressed them against his. As I rhythmically rocked against him, the boner in his jeans grew hard and long. He held perfectly still, his arms at his sides, letting me make all the moves.

I wondered as I ran my tongue over his lips, ignoring the annoying prickle and tickle of his coarse beard, for just a second, I wondered if his long, hard reaction to me was purely automatic. A simple trick of nature. He was unnaturally still.

I teased his mouth open with my tongue. He groaned and wrapped his arms around me, pulling me tightly against him as he arched up into me. His jeans were rough against the thin barrier of my silk panties.

His kiss was hard and inexperienced against mine. But damningly eager and enthusiastic. Almost endearing.

As his hands slid up my waist, hot on my back, tugging at my blouse, Data barked. And barked, dancing around us. *Jealous girl.*

I ignored her. We ignored her. I pushed Justin. Pushed myself. Pushed aside the racing of my pulse. The wetness of my panties. And the thought that there was any way I could possibly be turned on by him. There was no chemistry. There couldn't be. There never had been before. I must just be desperate. Distraught. Stressed. Tired.

He stuck his tongue deep in my mouth with the erotic intensity of a novice.

Data barked louder and jumped up at his legs, pawing and begging to be let up.

"Justin!" His name on her lips brought us up cold.

He froze. I pulled away and looked up across the room at a nerdy young woman, wearing a dress that looked like it belonged on her mom, or maybe her great grandmother, standing in the entry. At first glance, dressed in those matronly, boxy clothes, she could have been anywhere between twenty and fifty-five. She obviously had a key that let her all the way to the penthouse.

"Ophelia." His voice cracked. He looked as guilty as if she was the wronged party here. As if she'd actually caught us in bed.

Ophelia was definitely not so fair. Her face was dark and stormy. Her eyes were flashing and shining with hurt.

She's in love with him, I thought. *Oh, damn, she hates me on sight. And she's in love with my husband. Isn't this a lovely cliché?*

Gina Robinson is the award-winning author of the contemporary new adult romances *Rushed*, *Crushed*, *Reckless Longing*, *Reckless Secrets*, and *Reckless Together* and the Agent Ex series of humorous romantic suspense novels. She's currently working on the next installment of Switched at Marriage.

Connect with Gina Online:
My Website: http://www.ginarobinson.com/
Twitter: @ginamrobinson
Facebook: www.facebook.com/GinaRobinsonAuthor